This book of silly stories
and rhymes belongs to

_____

Silly Stories

Backpack Books
122 Fifth Avenue
New York, NY 10011

ISBN 0-7607-4648-6

Printed and bound in Indonesia

05 06 07 08 MCH 10 9 8 7 6 5 4 3

Produced by
The Templar Company plc

Silly Stories

Written by
Andy Charman, Heather Henning, Beatrice Phillpotts,
Caroline Repchuk, Louisa Somerville and Christine Tagg

Illustrated by
Diana Catchpole, Robin Edmonds, Chris Forsey
and Claire Mumford

BACKPACKBOOKS
o
NEW YORK

Contents

The Incredible Centipede

Clumsy Fred

Bumping into castles,
Turning homes to rubble,
Clumsy one-eyed monster Fred
Is a load of trouble.

Ooops! There goes a lamppost!
Help! A flying shed!
When careless Fred comes into town
It fills them all with dread.

But why is Fred so clumsy?
Has he gone quite mad?
Or has the friendly monster
Just suddenly turned bad?

We must stop that creature!
But how to save the day?
A monster expert took control:
"We'll do it all my way!"

The expert went to see him.
"I do need help," he cried.
"Why am I so clumsy?
It makes me sad," he sighed.

The expert did a lot of tests,
And then he gave a cry—
"I know what's wrong with you," he said.
"The problem is your eye!"

So Fred put on a monocle,
And suddenly could see.
He wasn't clumsy anymore,
He was happy as could be!

Denture Adventure

Grandpa's teeth grinned broadly as they sat in the glass on the bedside table, next to his glasses and a bowl of peanuts. Grandpa snored while a large African Gray Parrot sat on the brass headboard directly above Grandpa's head. At precisely seven-thirty it opened its beak and screeched, "Wakey, wakey," very, very loudly. Grandpa stretched out his hand and, without opening his eyes, patted the parrot on the head. The parrot was quiet for exactly nine minutes and then he began again.

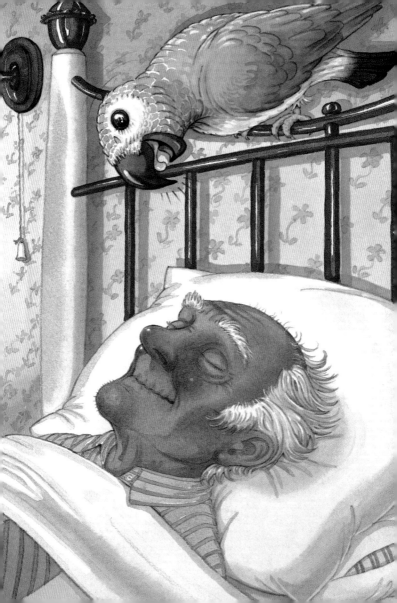

"Wakey, wakey," he called in a deafening screech. This continued until seven-fifty-seven, when Grandpa sat up in bed, yawned a gummy yawn and handed the parrot a peanut.

Grandpa stumbled out of bed, put on his slippers, and tripped across the hall to the bathroom. A face not unlike that of a turtle gazed back at him from the mirror, a turtle in Grandpa's striped pajamas. "Oh dear, oh dear," he said, gazing at his curious reflection. "Better put my teeth in."

Back in Grandpa's bedroom, Norman the African Gray parrot had similar thoughts, and was sitting proudly on the headboard sporting Grandpa's false teeth. He had helped himself to them from the glass while Grandpa had been in the bathroom.

"Who's a pretty boy?" he screeched and the

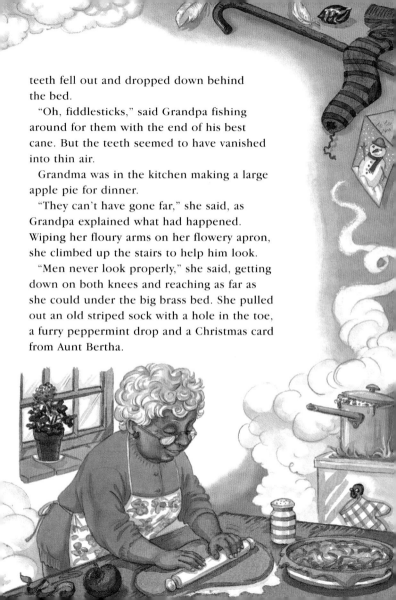

teeth fell out and dropped down behind
the bed.

"Oh, fiddlesticks," said Grandpa fishing
around for them with the end of his best
cane. But the teeth seemed to have vanished
into thin air.

Grandma was in the kitchen making a large
apple pie for dinner.

"They can't have gone far," she said, as
Grandpa explained what had happened.
Wiping her floury arms on her flowery apron,
she climbed up the stairs to help him look.

"Men never look properly," she said, getting
down on both knees and reaching as far as
she could under the big brass bed. She pulled
out an old striped sock with a hole in the toe,
a furry peppermint drop and a Christmas card
from Aunt Bertha.

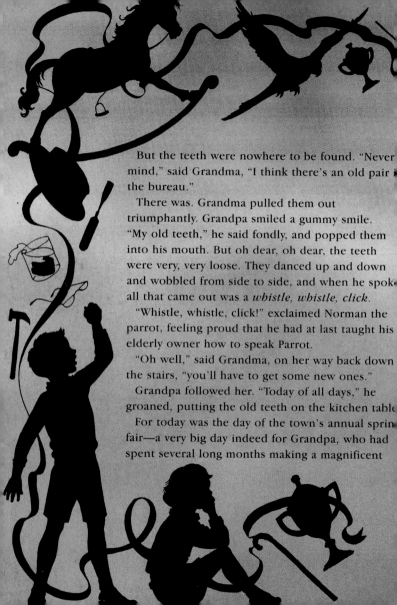

But the teeth were nowhere to be found. "Never mind," said Grandma, "I think there's an old pair i the bureau."

There was. Grandma pulled them out triumphantly. Grandpa smiled a gummy smile. "My old teeth," he said fondly, and popped them into his mouth. But oh dear, oh dear, the teeth were very, very loose. They danced up and down and wobbled from side to side, and when he spok all that came out was a *whistle, whistle, click*.

"Whistle, whistle, click!" exclaimed Norman the parrot, feeling proud that he had at last taught his elderly owner how to speak Parrot.

"Oh well," said Grandma, on her way back down the stairs, "you'll have to get some new ones."

Grandpa followed her. "Today of all days," he groaned, putting the old teeth on the kitchen table

For today was the day of the town's annual sprin fair—a very big day indeed for Grandpa, who had spent several long months making a magnificent

rocking horse, which he had entered in
one of the craft exhibits.

"You'll just have to not smile today," suggested
Grandma not very helpfully as she lay a large
pastry blanket over the fat wedges of juicy apple.
"Or talk," she added. Grandpa shrugged his
narrow shoulders and ambled over to his potting
shed, feeling fairly sorry for himself.

"Hmm, I wonder," said Grandma as she gazed
at the false teeth sitting on the edge of her table.
She picked them up thoughtfully, and then very
carefully and very neatly, she crimped the edge
of her apple pie with them. Grandpa stood in his
shed flicking a feather dust over the shiny
dappled neck of his fine rocking horse. He stood
back to admire his work. The horse was perfect
in every detail. A real leather saddle and bridle, a
silken mane and tail, neat glossy black hoofs and
two large brown eyes with wonderful long lashes.
Grandpa rubbed his bristly chin and frowned.

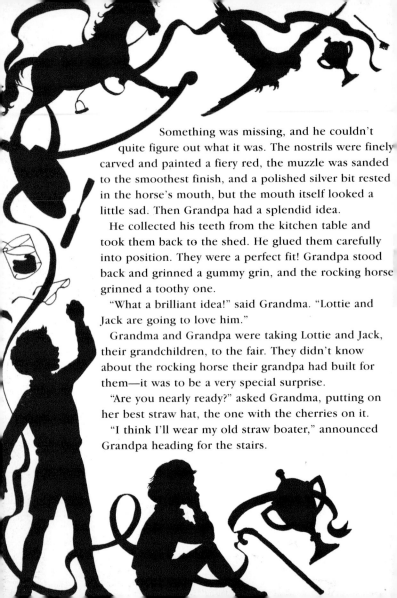

Something was missing, and he couldn't quite figure out what it was. The nostrils were finely carved and painted a fiery red, the muzzle was sanded to the smoothest finish, and a polished silver bit rested in the horse's mouth, but the mouth itself looked a little sad. Then Grandpa had a splendid idea.

He collected his teeth from the kitchen table and took them back to the shed. He glued them carefully into position. They were a perfect fit! Grandpa stood back and grinned a gummy grin, and the rocking horse grinned a toothy one.

"What a brilliant idea!" said Grandma. "Lottie and Jack are going to love him."

Grandma and Grandpa were taking Lottie and Jack, their grandchildren, to the fair. They didn't know about the rocking horse their grandpa had built for them—it was to be a very special surprise.

"Are you nearly ready?" asked Grandma, putting on her best straw hat, the one with the cherries on it.

"I think I'll wear my old straw boater," announced Grandpa heading for the stairs.

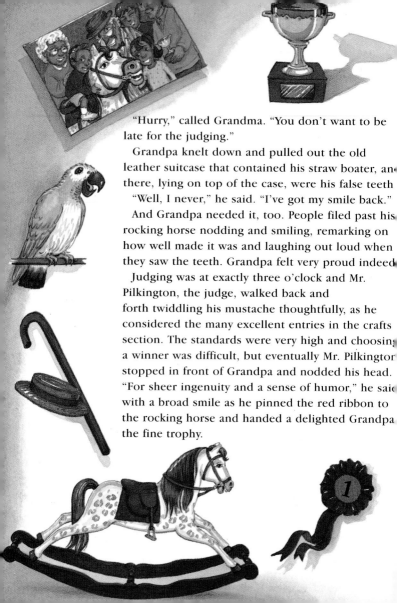

"Hurry," called Grandma. "You don't want to be late for the judging."

Grandpa knelt down and pulled out the old leather suitcase that contained his straw boater, and there, lying on top of the case, were his false teeth.

"Well, I never," he said. "I've got my smile back."

And Grandpa needed it, too. People filed past his rocking horse nodding and smiling, remarking on how well made it was and laughing out loud when they saw the teeth. Grandpa felt very proud indeed.

Judging was at exactly three o'clock and Mr. Pilkington, the judge, walked back and forth twiddling his mustache thoughtfully, as he considered the many excellent entries in the crafts section. The standards were very high and choosing a winner was difficult, but eventually Mr. Pilkington stopped in front of Grandpa and nodded his head. "For sheer ingenuity and a sense of humor," he said with a broad smile as he pinned the red ribbon to the rocking horse and handed a delighted Grandpa the fine trophy.

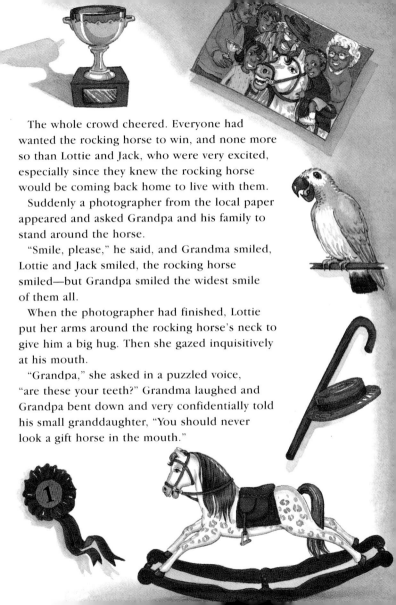

The whole crowd cheered. Everyone had
wanted the rocking horse to win, and none more
so than Lottie and Jack, who were very excited,
especially since they knew the rocking horse
would be coming back home to live with them.

Suddenly a photographer from the local paper
appeared and asked Grandpa and his family to
stand around the horse.

"Smile, please," he said, and Grandma smiled,
Lottie and Jack smiled, the rocking horse
smiled—but Grandpa smiled the widest smile
of them all.

When the photographer had finished, Lottie
put her arms around the rocking horse's neck to
give him a big hug. Then she gazed inquisitively
at his mouth.

"Grandpa," she asked in a puzzled voice,
"are these your teeth?" Grandma laughed and
Grandpa bent down and very confidentially told
his small granddaughter, "You should never
look a gift horse in the mouth."

My Funny Family

My aunt May's got a brain like a sieve—
She forgets where the things in her kitchen live.
There are plates in the fridge and chops in the drawers
Carrots in the mugs and hot dogs hung on doors.

My uncle Fred's got ears like cauliflowers—
He listens to the neighbors chat for hours and hours and hours
He can hear an ant whistling from a mile away or more,
And butterflies who flutter and ladybugs who snore!

My cousin Bob's got eyes like a hawk—
He can see all the way from Chicago to New York!
He says he can see planets orbiting in space,
And that the moon has a handlebar mustache upon its face.

My sister Sarah's got feet that love to dance—
She's danced from Perth to Benidorm, from Italy to France.
She dances in a dress trimmed with black and yellow lace,
Mom says she looks just like a bee and that it's a disgrace!

My brother Tom's got tricks up his sleeve—
He's got creepy things and spiders, and bugs to make you heave.
He once flicked a baked bean, which fell on Grandpa's head
And poor Grandpa didn't know until he went to bed!

My dog Jasper's got a ferocious appetite—
To see him gobbling up his food is really quite a sight.
He wolfs down spaghetti and when he's really feeling gross,
He'll polish off a cake and a pile of buttered toast!

The Powerful Spell

The sky turned black and the villagers ran for their lives. "Help! Help!" they cried, as they dashed for the safety of the castle. "The dragon is back!" A huge shape swooped down, blotting out the sun, as the last villager flung himself inside, puffing and panting. The heavy castle doors, made of solid steel, clanged shut, and the mighty bridge across the moat was drawn up.

Hovering above the thick stone castle roof and walls, its giant green, scaly wings outstretched, was a huge and terrible dragon—the enemy of the village.

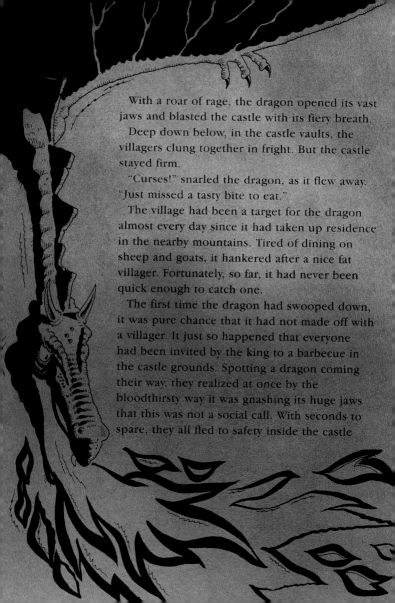

With a roar of rage, the dragon opened its vast jaws and blasted the castle with its fiery breath.

Deep down below, in the castle vaults, the villagers clung together in fright. But the castle stayed firm.

"Curses!" snarled the dragon, as it flew away. "Just missed a tasty bite to eat."

The village had been a target for the dragon almost every day since it had taken up residence in the nearby mountains. Tired of dining on sheep and goats, it hankered after a nice fat villager. Fortunately, so far, it had never been quick enough to catch one.

The first time the dragon had swooped down, it was pure chance that it had not made off with a villager. It just so happened that everyone had been invited by the king to a barbecue in the castle grounds. Spotting a dragon coming their way, they realized at once by the bloodthirsty way it was gnashing its huge jaws that this was not a social call. With seconds to spare, they all fled to safety inside the castle

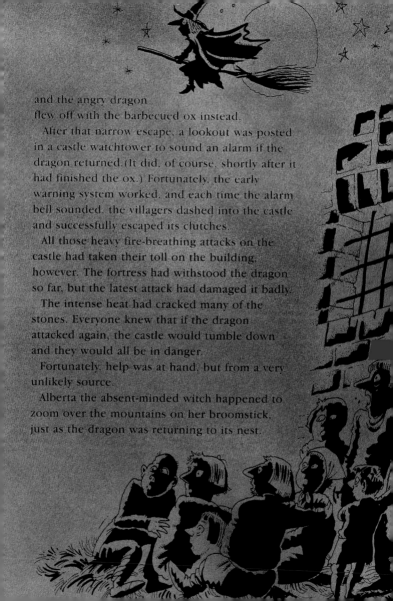

and the angry dragon
flew off with the barbecued ox instead.

After that narrow escape, a lookout was posted
in a castle watchtower to sound an alarm if the
dragon returned.(It did, of course, shortly after it
had finished the ox.) Fortunately, the early
warning system worked, and each time the alarm
bell sounded, the villagers dashed into the castle
and successfully escaped its clutches.

All those heavy fire-breathing attacks on the
castle had taken their toll on the building,
however. The fortress had withstood the dragon
so far, but the latest attack had damaged it badly.

The intense heat had cracked many of the
stones. Everyone knew that if the dragon
attacked again, the castle would tumble down
and they would all be in danger.

Fortunately, help was at hand, but from a very
unlikely source.

Alberta the absent-minded witch happened to
zoom over the mountains on her broomstick,
just as the dragon was returning to its nest.

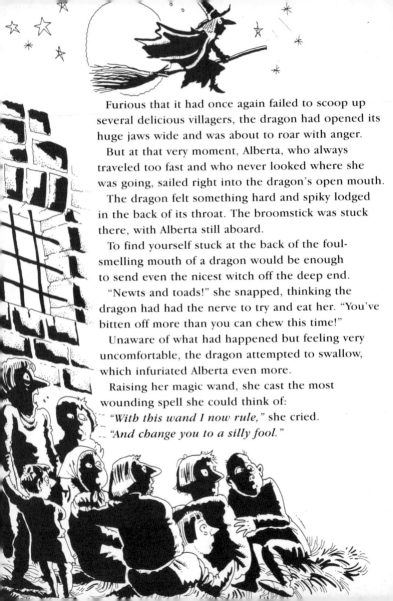

Furious that it had once again failed to scoop up several delicious villagers, the dragon had opened its huge jaws wide and was about to roar with anger.

But at that very moment, Alberta, who always traveled too fast and who never looked where she was going, sailed right into the dragon's open mouth.

The dragon felt something hard and spiky lodged in the back of its throat. The broomstick was stuck there, with Alberta still aboard.

To find yourself stuck at the back of the foul-smelling mouth of a dragon would be enough to send even the nicest witch off the deep end.

"Newts and toads!" she snapped, thinking the dragon had had the nerve to try and eat her. "You've bitten off more than you can chew this time!"

Unaware of what had happened but feeling very uncomfortable, the dragon attempted to swallow, which infuriated Alberta even more.

Raising her magic wand, she cast the most wounding spell she could think of:

"With this wand I now rule," she cried.
"And change you to a silly fool."

Then she conjured herself back to the comfort of her own home for a little rest and a restorative cup of slime tea.

Blissfully ignorant of the fact that a powerful spell had been cast upon it, the dragon returned to its nest. It was relieved that whatever had gotten stuck in its throat was no longer there, and had no idea that it had been a witch.

Later that day, however, it felt a little hungry.

"I'll show those villagers this time," the dragon promised itself, as it set off in search of tasty humans once again.

But little did the dragon realize exactly what kind of a show it would be putting on.

"Dragon ahoy!" shouted the look out sounding the alarm bell as the familiar giant black shape appeared in the sky.

The whole village was panic-stricken. They knew that the badly damaged castle wouldn't withstand another firebombing. If it tumbled down, the dragon would gobble them all up.

But there was nowhere else to run.
So, preparing themselves for the worst,
they shut themselves up inside it as usual.
Hidden well away from the huge holes in the
roof, they clung to each other for comfort and
prayed that somehow they would be saved.

And astonishingly enough, they were.

The dreadful beating noise made by the
dragon's vast wings came nearer and nearer. The
blue sky visible through the gaping holes in the
ceiling went black, as the dragon hovered
overhead. But the dreaded fiery jets of dragon
breath never came.

When the enchanted dragon drew a deep
breath and blew out with all its might, no sheets
of flame shot out. Instead, millions of sweet-
smelling flower petals fluttered downward
from its gaping jaws.

The villagers stared in amazement as pretty
petals floated through the holes above their
heads and gathered in drifts around their feet.

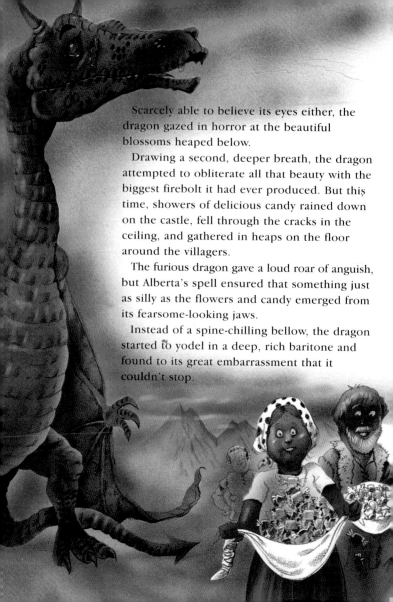

Scarcely able to believe its eyes either, the dragon gazed in horror at the beautiful blossoms heaped below.

Drawing a second, deeper breath, the dragon attempted to obliterate all that beauty with the biggest firebolt it had ever produced. But this time, showers of delicious candy rained down on the castle, fell through the cracks in the ceiling, and gathered in heaps on the floor around the villagers.

The furious dragon gave a loud roar of anguish, but Alberta's spell ensured that something just as silly as the flowers and candy emerged from its fearsome-looking jaws.

Instead of a spine-chilling bellow, the dragon started to yodel in a deep, rich baritone and found to its great embarrassment that it couldn't stop.

"I love you-ee-ou-ee-ou-ee-ou," it sang to the astonished villagers.

Inside the castle, everyone started to laugh. As the dragon continued to yodel a love song to them, they laughed even harder.

The dragon knew it was making a ridiculous spectacle of itself but thanks to Alberta's spell, it couldn't do anything about it.

Well, it could do something, the dragon realized. It could fly away and never come back.

And that is exactly what the dragon did.

"Good riddance to you, you silly fool," the king called after the dragon as it flew off over the castle walls as quickly as it could, still singing at the top of its voice.

Then everyone enjoyed a wonderful feast of candy, before they rebuilt the castle and lived happily ever after.

The Incredible Centipede

I'm not just an ordinary centipede,
  I live in a circus van,
  I know all the top performers,
And I have a wonderful plan...

We'll reach a town, and as the sun goes down,
The folks will crowd the tent;
With music to thrill, they'll pick up the bill
And read with astonishment:

"Star of the show in the ring tonight,
And we hope he does succeed,
Is the enterprising, most surprising,
Incredible Centipede!"

The curtains will part and out I'll dart
And shake a leg or six,
Then in spangled tights I'll scale the heights
To perform my amazing tricks.

I'll swing from the wire with a toehold catch
And fold my legs like a clown;
I'll pedal the bike with the balancing pole,
But I'll ride it upside down!

I'll fly though the air without a net—
They'll be standing on their seats.
The crowds will roar, they'll be calling for more
Of my incredible feats.

It will be so grand, in every land,
Royalty will want to be seen
Meeting the Incredible Centipede—
And I'll meet lots of kings and queens.

The Incredible Centipede

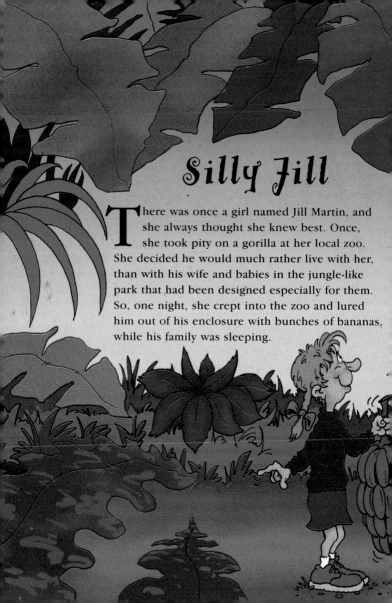

Silly Jill

There was once a girl named Jill Martin, and
she always thought she knew best. Once,
she took pity on a gorilla at her local zoo.
She decided he would much rather live with her,
than with his wife and babies in the jungle-like
park that had been designed especially for them.
So, one night, she crept into the zoo and lured
him out of his enclosure with bunches of bananas,
while his family was sleeping.

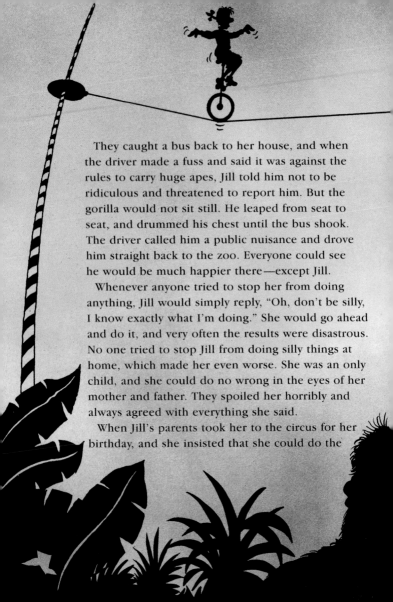

They caught a bus back to her house, and when the driver made a fuss and said it was against the rules to carry huge apes, Jill told him not to be ridiculous and threatened to report him. But the gorilla would not sit still. He leaped from seat to seat, and drummed his chest until the bus shook. The driver called him a public nuisance and drove him straight back to the zoo. Everyone could see he would be much happier there—except Jill.

Whenever anyone tried to stop her from doing anything, Jill would simply reply, "Oh, don't be silly, I know exactly what I'm doing." She would go ahead and do it, and very often the results were disastrous. No one tried to stop Jill from doing silly things at home, which made her even worse. She was an only child, and she could do no wrong in the eyes of her mother and father. They spoiled her horribly and always agreed with everything she said.

When Jill's parents took her to the circus for her birthday, and she insisted that she could do the

high-wire act better than the acrobats, her mother and
father just said "Of course you can, darling."

If another child had told her parents that they
probably wouldn't have really meant it. But Jill was
truly convinced that she could somersault from the
trapeze and ride a unicycle across the high-wire. Other
parents would have tried to stop their child from
trying anything that dangerous. But Jill's parents were
just as silly as Jill. So they let her try.

The ringmaster tried to stop them. He cracked his
whip and twirled his mustache furiously, but Jill's
parents were determined to let their daughter do what
she wanted to do. They were so insistent and offered
him so much money, that finally he did.

It was bound to be a disaster, as anyone could have
told Jill. In fact, it was a hilarious disaster. She did
everything so horribly wrong, it looked like a comedy
routine. She flew backwards off the unicycle as it
gathered speed along the high wire, looped the loop,
and landed in the arms of a clown.

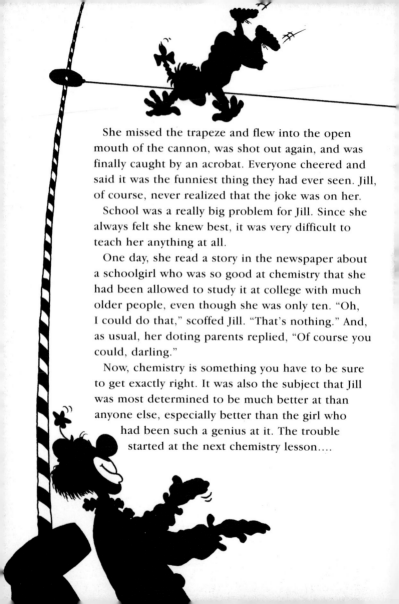

She missed the trapeze and flew into the open mouth of the cannon, was shot out again, and was finally caught by an acrobat. Everyone cheered and said it was the funniest thing they had ever seen. Jill, of course, never realized that the joke was on her.

School was a really big problem for Jill. Since she always felt she knew best, it was very difficult to teach her anything at all.

One day, she read a story in the newspaper about a schoolgirl who was so good at chemistry that she had been allowed to study it at college with much older people, even though she was only ten. "Oh, I could do that," scoffed Jill. "That's nothing." And, as usual, her doting parents replied, "Of course you could, darling."

Now, chemistry is something you have to be sure to get exactly right. It was also the subject that Jill was most determined to be much better at than anyone else, especially better than the girl who had been such a genius at it. The trouble started at the next chemistry lesson....

The rest of the class listened carefully to the chemistry teacher. She explained that in their next experiment it was very important not to mix the wrong liquids. Under no circumstances should blue be mixed with red.

"Hah!" thought Jill. "I'll bet it works much better if you mix the blue with the red." And so, without anyone seeing, she mixed blue and red.

Bang! Jill's flask exploded the instant they were combined, and a stream of foul-smelling, smoking purple liquid poured onto the floor.

"You silly, silly girl!" shouted the chemistry teacher. "What have you done?"

It was difficult to see exactly what Jill had done, the classroom was so full of smoke.

But everyone started to feel what she had done almost immediately.

"Help!" they shouted, as one by one, they felt themselves being lifted off the floor.

A really extraordinary thing had happened. The spilled liquid had made something like grass grow out of the floor. Only, instead of growing slowly like grass usually does, this stuff was growing upward in leaps and bounds, like a meadow that had gone mad.

"Head for the door!" screamed the chemistry teacher, as the long waving carpet of grass carried them all up toward the ceiling. It was almost like being on a roller coaster.

So they all went, even Jill. They crawled across the narrow space that was still left as fast as they could, trying not to bang their heads on the lights, while the grassy carpet shot upward in a huge mass.

Then, just before they reached the door, the grassy carpet flowered. Fat buds burst out into brightly colored blooms. Everyone who had hay fever started spluttering and sneezing.

Luckily, the classroom door was open. They squeezed their way out before the grassy carpet filled the room, and then tumbled out into the corridor, chasing the last children out of the door.

"Run for it!" commanded the teacher, pressing the fire alarm to alert the rest of the school. And eight hundred children, including Jill, thirty teachers, the caretaker and the cat raced for the safety of the school yard, just before the school was completely swallowed up by a carpet of grass.

It took every fire fighter in town a week to cut the carpet down, and for months afterward it still sprouted the occasional flower.

The school had to be closed, of course, while the giant carpet was cut, mowed, rolled, and finally brought under control. The principal was furious with Jill when she heard how it had all started.

"Your silly, thoughtless behavior could have destroyed this school and everyone in it," she told her. "I hope this has taught you a lesson and you know now that you do not always know better than anyone else."

Fortunately for Jill—and the school—it had taught her a lesson that she never forgot. From that dreadful day on, she stopped insisting she knew best, and to everyone's relief, there were no more disasters.

In fact, Jill's terrible mistake turned out to be a fantastic opportunity for the school. A high-ranking army officer heard about Jill's silly experiment and the amazing result. He decided that a quick-growing carpet would be an excellent weapon. He paid the school a lot of money for the details of Jill's purple mixture. This meant that the school was able to build a swimming pool, ice rink and bowling alley for the whole town to use. And it wasn't long before Jill mended her ways and really did become a star pupil—but everyone still knew her as Silly Jill!

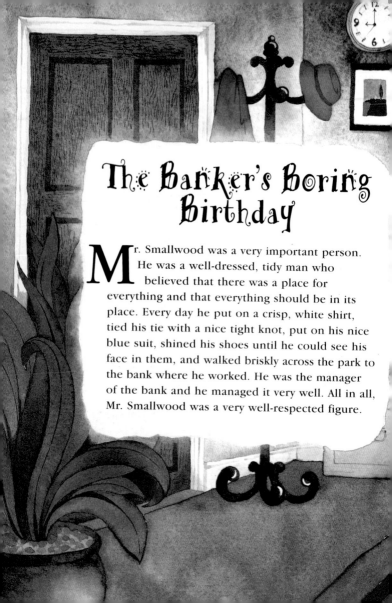

The Banker's Boring Birthday

Mr. Smallwood was a very important person. He was a well-dressed, tidy man who believed that there was a place for everything and that everything should be in its place. Every day he put on a crisp, white shirt, tied his tie with a nice tight knot, put on his nice blue suit, shined his shoes until he could see his face in them, and walked briskly across the park to the bank where he worked. He was the manager of the bank and he managed it very well. All in all, Mr. Smallwood was a very well-respected figure.

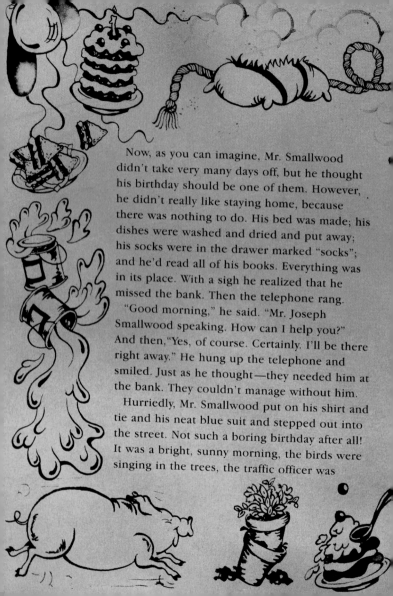

Now, as you can imagine, Mr. Smallwood didn't take very many days off, but he thought his birthday should be one of them. However, he didn't really like staying home, because there was nothing to do. His bed was made; his dishes were washed and dried and put away; his socks were in the drawer marked "socks"; and he'd read all of his books. Everything was in its place. With a sigh he realized that he missed the bank. Then the telephone rang.

"Good morning," he said. "Mr. Joseph Smallwood speaking. How can I help you?" And then, "Yes, of course. Certainly. I'll be there right away." He hung up the telephone and smiled. Just as he thought—they needed him at the bank. They couldn't manage without him.

Hurriedly, Mr. Smallwood put on his shirt and tie and his neat blue suit and stepped out into the street. Not such a boring birthday after all! It was a bright, sunny morning, the birds were singing in the trees, the traffic officer was

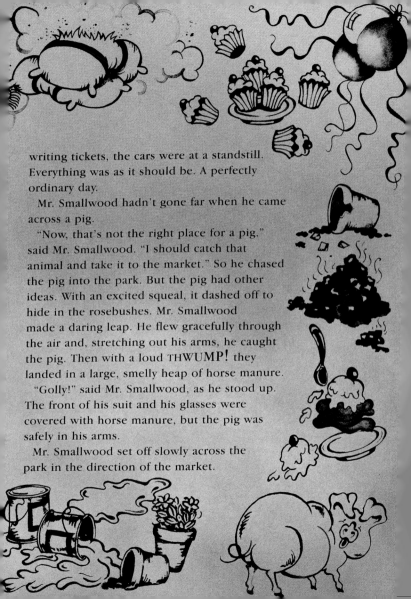

writing tickets, the cars were at a standstill.
Everything was as it should be. A perfectly
ordinary day.

Mr. Smallwood hadn't gone far when he came
across a pig.

"Now, that's not the right place for a pig,"
said Mr. Smallwood. "I should catch that
animal and take it to the market." So he chased
the pig into the park. But the pig had other
ideas. With an excited squeal, it dashed off to
hide in the rosebushes. Mr. Smallwood
made a daring leap. He flew gracefully through
the air and, stretching out his arms, he caught
the pig. Then with a loud THWUMP! they
landed in a large, smelly heap of horse manure.

"Golly!" said Mr. Smallwood, as he stood up.
The front of his suit and his glasses were
covered with horse manure, but the pig was
safely in his arms.

Mr. Smallwood set off slowly across the
park in the direction of the market.

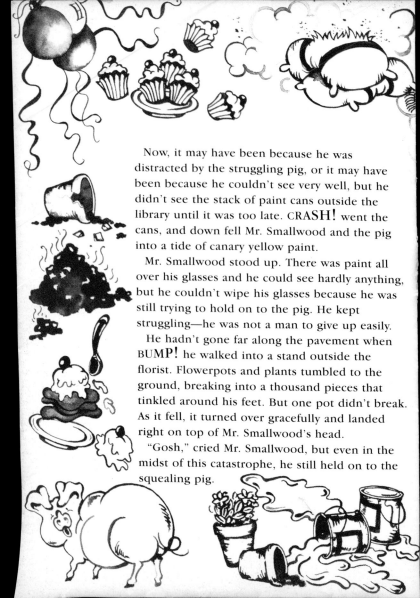

Now, it may have been because he was distracted by the struggling pig, or it may have been because he couldn't see very well, but he didn't see the stack of paint cans outside the library until it was too late. CRASH! went the cans, and down fell Mr. Smallwood and the pig into a tide of canary yellow paint.

Mr. Smallwood stood up. There was paint all over his glasses and he could see hardly anything, but he couldn't wipe his glasses because he was still trying to hold on to the pig. He kept struggling—he was not a man to give up easily.

He hadn't gone far along the pavement when BUMP! he walked into a stand outside the florist. Flowerpots and plants tumbled to the ground, breaking into a thousand pieces that tinkled around his feet. But one pot didn't break. As it fell, it turned over gracefully and landed right on top of Mr. Smallwood's head.

"Gosh," cried Mr. Smallwood, but even in the midst of this catastrophe, he still held on to the squealing pig.

Staggering slightly and a little dazed, Mr. Smallwood walked on. He hadn't gone very far when a voice cried, "LOOK OUT!" He walked straight into Claude, the waiter at the Crêpe Café. Claude was serving pancakes and ice cream to some customers, but they didn't get them. Down went Claude, up in the air went his tray, and SLAP! two pancakes landed squarely on Mr. Smallwood's shiny shoes.

Always a polite man, Mr Smallwood turned to apologize to Claude and his customers. "Sorry!" he called out. But before he knew what was happening he was falling, stumbling backwards into a hole full of muddy water on a construction site.

"Golly," said Mr. Smallwood, and, still holding firmly on to the pig, he pulled himself out of the hole. Now, maybe it was because he was tired by now and not concentrating, or maybe it was because he had manure and paint and mud on his glasses, but Mr. Smallwood didn't realize that he was on a construction site. He also didn't realize that he was pulling himself up by a rope attached to a pile of cement bags. The pile swayed, the pile wobbled. The top bag slid off and exploded majestically over Mr. Smallwood's head, covering him in a cloud of cement dust.

Mr Smallwood coughed, wheezed, and spluttered as the cloud gradually cleared.

The cement began to harden as it soaked into Mr. Smallwood's damp suit. He walked away stiffly.

He hadn't gone far when he heard a familiar voice calling his name.

"Mr. Smallwood! There you are! We were wondering where you were." It was Mrs. Tillhead, the assistant bank manager.

Tired and a little shaken, Mr. Smallwood allowed himself to be led into the bank. As soon as he entered the building, a cheer went up.

"Hurrah," he heard, and "Happy Birthday!" Someone removed his glasses and cleaned them for him, and he looked around the room. The ceiling was hung with brightly colored streamers and balloons.

Above the tellers' windows was a huge banner with the words "HAPPY BIRTHDAY Mr. SMALLWOOD," and a table was bending under the weight of chips, sandwiches, and cake. All his employees had thrown a surprise birthday party for him!

Mr. Smallwood was very surprised, but not as surprised as everyone else!

Instead of seeing the small, dapper banker they expected and respected, they saw in front of them a man walking stiffly in a cement-covered suit, with a flowerpot on his head, pancakes draped over his shoes, smelling very strongly of horse manure and carrying a yellow, wriggling pig in his arms.

"Golly!" they cried.

The Land Where Animals Rule

In the land where the animals rule,
The children don't go to school.
They live on farms, and flap their arms,
Just like the chickens used to do.

The post-bears always wear blue,
It's faster on four legs than two.
But it's always better to send things by letter,
Because packages tend to get chewed.

Jaguars and speeding cheetahs,
Are stopped when they go too fast
By policing cats, in pointed hats,
And pandas in polka-dot cars.

Horses take themselves for a ride,
They trot down the road side by side.
In the carriages they own they travel alone—
There's no room for two on the inside.

In restaurants where herbivores go,
They never eat meat, so I'm told.
Cows do the cooking while no one is looking—
It's grass, and it's usually cold.

If you go for a round-the-world sail
You travel on the back of a whale.
Hold on for dear life when he starts to dive,
And look out for that oversized tail.

It's fun where the animals rule,
No one tells you what you ought to do.
Their idea of fun is to sleep in the sun,
It's just the place for a person like you.

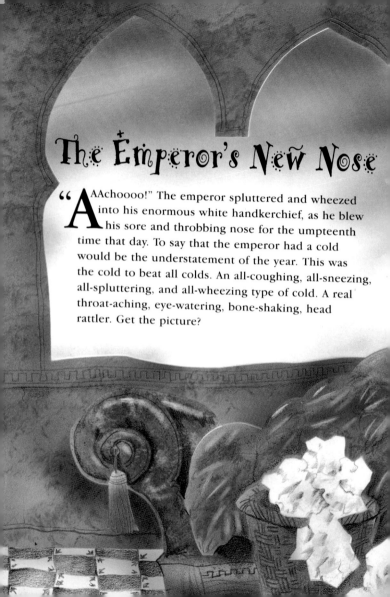

The Emperor's New Nose

"AAAchoooo!" The emperor spluttered and wheezed into his enormous white handkerchief, as he blew his sore and throbbing nose for the umpteenth time that day. To say that the emperor had a cold would be the understatement of the year. This was the cold to beat all colds. An all-coughing, all-sneezing, all-spluttering, and all-wheezing type of cold. A real throat-aching, eye-watering, bone-shaking, head rattler. Get the picture?

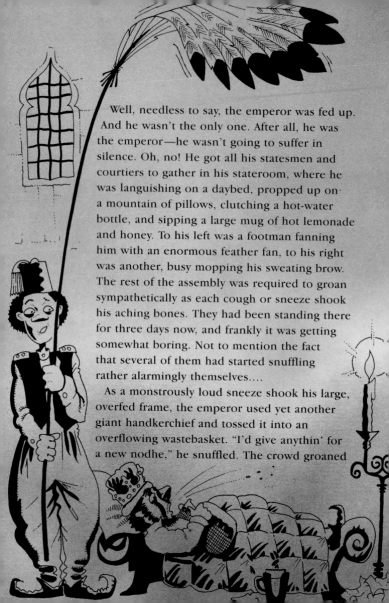

Well, needless to say, the emperor was fed up.
And he wasn't the only one. After all, he was
the emperor—he wasn't going to suffer in
silence. Oh, no! He got all his statesmen and
courtiers to gather in his stateroom, where he
was languishing on a daybed, propped up on
a mountain of pillows, clutching a hot-water
bottle, and sipping a large mug of hot lemonade
and honey. To his left was a footman fanning
him with an enormous feather fan, to his right
was another, busy mopping his sweating brow.
The rest of the assembly was required to groan
sympathetically as each cough or sneeze shook
his aching bones. They had been standing there
for three days now, and frankly it was getting
somewhat boring. Not to mention the fact
that several of them had started snuffling
rather alarmingly themselves….

As a monstrously loud sneeze shook his large,
overfed frame, the emperor used yet another
giant handkerchief and tossed it into an
overflowing wastebasket. "I'd give anythin' for
a new nodhe," he snuffled. The crowd groaned

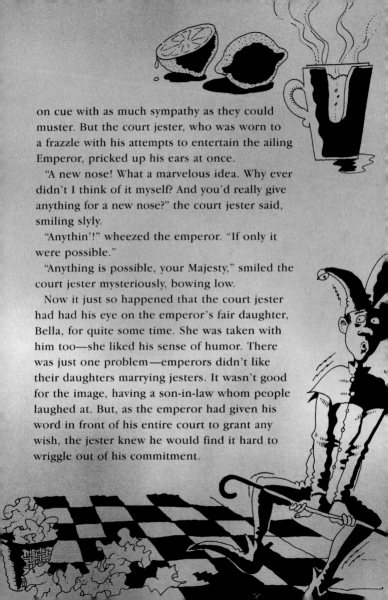

on cue with as much sympathy as they could muster. But the court jester, who was worn to a frazzle with his attempts to entertain the ailing Emperor, pricked up his ears at once.

"A new nose! What a marvelous idea. Why ever didn't I think of it myself? And you'd really give anything for a new nose?" the court jester said, smiling slyly.

"Anythin'!" wheezed the emperor. "If only it were possible."

"Anything is possible, your Majesty," smiled the court jester mysteriously, bowing low.

Now it just so happened that the court jester had had his eye on the emperor's fair daughter, Bella, for quite some time. She was taken with him too—she liked his sense of humor. There was just one problem—emperors didn't like their daughters marrying jesters. It wasn't good for the image, having a son-in-law whom people laughed at. But, as the emperor had given his word in front of his entire court to grant any wish, the jester knew he would find it hard to wriggle out of his commitment.

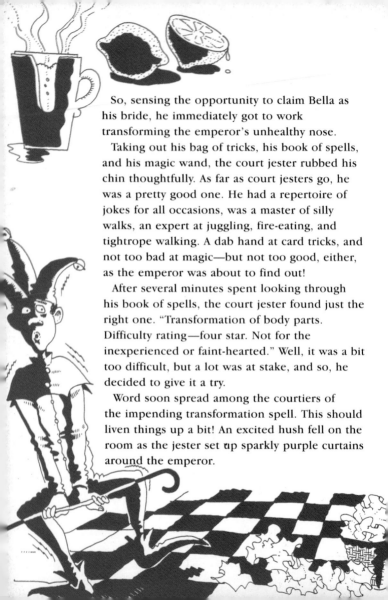

So, sensing the opportunity to claim Bella as his bride, he immediately got to work transforming the emperor's unhealthy nose.

Taking out his bag of tricks, his book of spells, and his magic wand, the court jester rubbed his chin thoughtfully. As far as court jesters go, he was a pretty good one. He had a repertoire of jokes for all occasions, was a master of silly walks, an expert at juggling, fire-eating, and tightrope walking. A dab hand at card tricks, and not too bad at magic—but not too good, either, as the emperor was about to find out!

After several minutes spent looking through his book of spells, the court jester found just the right one. "Transformation of body parts. Difficulty rating—four star. Not for the inexperienced or faint-hearted." Well, it was a bit too difficult, but a lot was at stake, and so, he decided to give it a try.

Word soon spread among the courtiers of the impending transformation spell. This should liven things up a bit! An excited hush fell on the room as the jester set up sparkly purple curtains around the emperor.

The jester paced up and down, muttering under his breath. He was deciding on the exact wording of the spell and practicing until he had it down pat. Then he picked up his wand, tapped it on his spell book, and asked for silence as he recited the magic words:

"Abracadabra, snuffles and wheezes,
Away with this nose with its splutters and sneezes.
Something grand and imposing appear in its place,
A noble nose, fit for a true leader's face!"

With that, he waved his wand in the air, making a trail of sparkling stars. Behind the screen, there was a bright green flash of light, and the audience let out a great gasp as the court jester pulled back the curtains to reveal the emperor with his new nose in all its glory. It was certainly grand, certainly imposing, and definitely fit for a noble leader—as long as he was leading a herd of elephants! For there, right in the middle of the

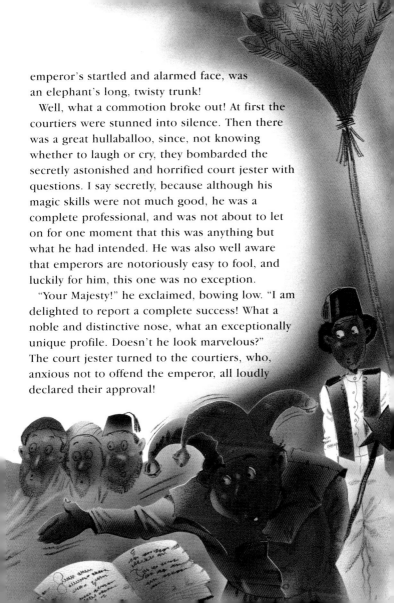

emperor's startled and alarmed face, was
an elephant's long, twisty trunk!

Well, what a commotion broke out! At first the
courtiers were stunned into silence. Then there
was a great hullaballoo, since, not knowing
whether to laugh or cry, they bombarded the
secretly astonished and horrified court jester with
questions. I say secretly, because although his
magic skills were not much good, he was a
complete professional, and was not about to let
on for one moment that this was anything but
what he had intended. He was also well aware
that emperors are notoriously easy to fool, and
luckily for him, this one was no exception.

"Your Majesty!" he exclaimed, bowing low. "I am
delighted to report a complete success! What a
noble and distinctive nose, what an exceptionally
unique profile. Doesn't he look marvelous?"
The court jester turned to the courtiers, who,
anxious not to offend the emperor, all loudly
declared their approval!

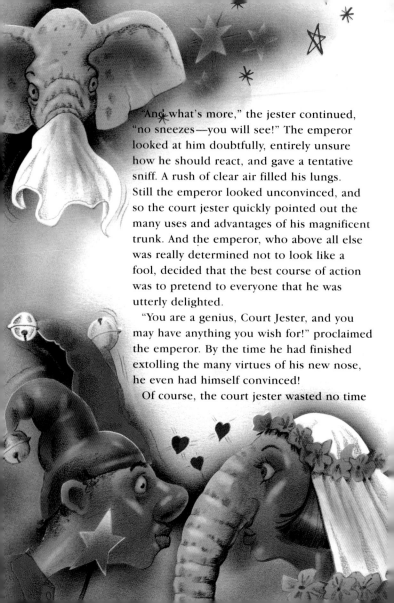

"And what's more," the jester continued, "no sneezes—you will see!" The emperor looked at him doubtfully, entirely unsure how he should react, and gave a tentative sniff. A rush of clear air filled his lungs. Still the emperor looked unconvinced, and so the court jester quickly pointed out the many uses and advantages of his magnificent trunk. And the emperor, who above all else was really determined not to look like a fool, decided that the best course of action was to pretend to everyone that he was utterly delighted.

"You are a genius, Court Jester, and you may have anything you wish for!" proclaimed the emperor. By the time he had finished extolling the many virtues of his new nose, he even had himself convinced!

Of course, the court jester wasted no time

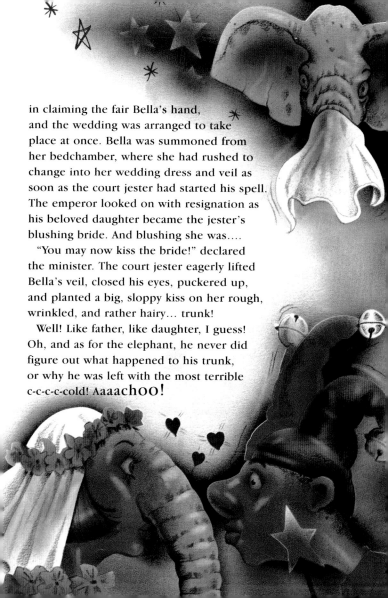

in claiming the fair Bella's hand, and the wedding was arranged to take place at once. Bella was summoned from her bedchamber, where she had rushed to change into her wedding dress and veil as soon as the court jester had started his spell. The emperor looked on with resignation as his beloved daughter became the jester's blushing bride. And blushing she was....

"You may now kiss the bride!" declared the minister. The court jester eagerly lifted Bella's veil, closed his eyes, puckered up, and planted a big, sloppy kiss on her rough, wrinkled, and rather hairy... trunk!

Well! Like father, like daughter, I guess! Oh, and as for the elephant, he never did figure out what happened to his trunk, or why he was left with the most terrible c-c-c-c-cold! Aaaachoo!

A Shipful of Fun

It was a wild, stormy night. Windows rattled and garbage can lids clattered down the narrow . streets Poppy sat wide awake in her bed, listening to the wind howling and the crashing waves. She wondered about the poor seagulls— where would they go on a night like this? Suddenly, her room was filled with bright orange light. A flare! Something was happening at sea! Poppy woke her father and they rushed down to the beach, pulling on their coats. People were appearing from everywhere and there was an air of anticipation as they all gathered on the beach—Poppy had the feeling it would be an eventful night.

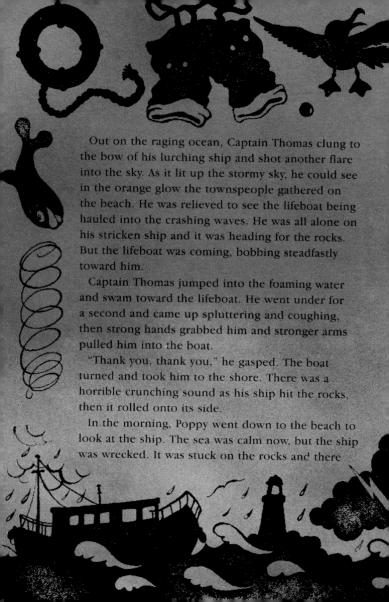

Out on the raging ocean, Captain Thomas clung to the bow of his lurching ship and shot another flare into the sky. As it lit up the stormy sky, he could see in the orange glow the townspeople gathered on the beach. He was relieved to see the lifeboat being hauled into the crashing waves. He was all alone on his stricken ship and it was heading for the rocks. But the lifeboat was coming, bobbing steadfastly toward him.

Captain Thomas jumped into the foaming water and swam toward the lifeboat. He went under for a second and came up spluttering and coughing, then strong hands grabbed him and stronger arms pulled him into the boat.

"Thank you, thank you," he gasped. The boat turned and took him to the shore. There was a horrible crunching sound as his ship hit the rocks, then it rolled onto its side.

In the morning, Poppy went down to the beach to look at the ship. The sea was calm now, but the ship was wrecked. It was stuck on the rocks and there

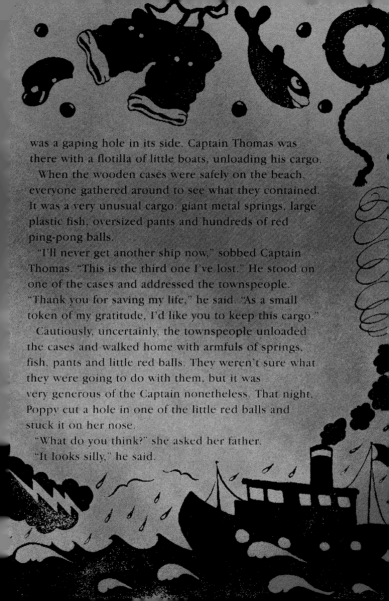

was a gaping hole in its side. Captain Thomas was there with a flotilla of little boats, unloading his cargo.

When the wooden cases were safely on the beach, everyone gathered around to see what they contained. It was a very unusual cargo: giant metal springs, large plastic fish, oversized pants and hundreds of red ping-pong balls.

"I'll never get another ship now," sobbed Captain Thomas. "This is the third one I've lost." He stood on one of the cases and addressed the townspeople. "Thank you for saving my life," he said. "As a small token of my gratitude, I'd like you to keep this cargo."

Cautiously, uncertainly, the townspeople unloaded the cases and walked home with armfuls of springs, fish, pants and little red balls. They weren't sure what they were going to do with them, but it was very generous of the Captain nonetheless. That night, Poppy cut a hole in one of the little red balls and stuck it on her nose.

"What do you think?" she asked her father.

"It looks silly," he said.

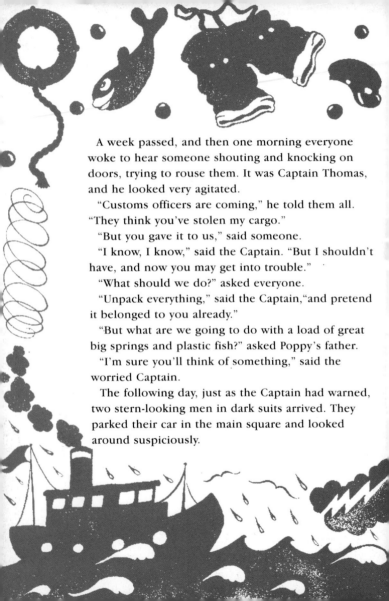

A week passed, and then one morning everyone woke to hear someone shouting and knocking on doors, trying to rouse them. It was Captain Thomas, and he looked very agitated.

"Customs officers are coming," he told them all. "They think you've stolen my cargo."

"But you gave it to us," said someone.

"I know, I know," said the Captain. "But I shouldn't have, and now you may get into trouble."

"What should we do?" asked everyone.

"Unpack everything," said the Captain, "and pretend it belonged to you already."

"But what are we going to do with a load of great big springs and plastic fish?" asked Poppy's father.

"I'm sure you'll think of something," said the worried Captain.

The following day, just as the Captain had warned, two stern-looking men in dark suits arrived. They parked their car in the main square and looked around suspiciously.

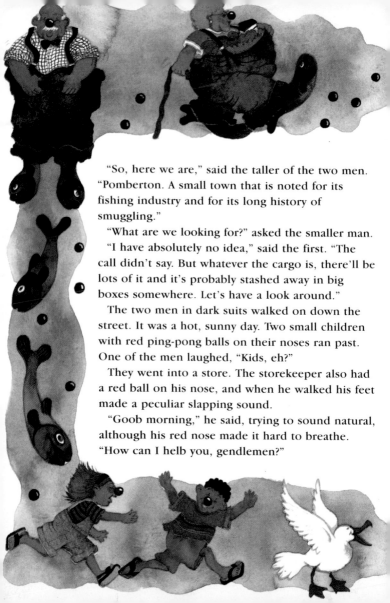

"So, here we are," said the taller of the two men. "Pomberton. A small town that is noted for its fishing industry and for its long history of smuggling."

"What are we looking for?" asked the smaller man.

"I have absolutely no idea," said the first. "The call didn't say. But whatever the cargo is, there'll be lots of it and it's probably stashed away in big boxes somewhere. Let's have a look around."

The two men in dark suits walked on down the street. It was a hot, sunny day. Two small children with red ping-pong balls on their noses ran past. One of the men laughed, "Kids, eh?"

They went into a store. The storekeeper also had a red ball on his nose, and when he walked his feet made a peculiar slapping sound.

"Goob morning," he said, trying to sound natural, although his red nose made it hard to breathe. "How can I helb you, gendlemen?"

"Customs officers," said the tall man, waving his badge in the man's face. "We'd like to have a look around if you don't mind."

"Helb yourself," said the storekeeper.

Just then an old woman, also wearing a red ball on her nose and a pair of enormous pants came into the shop. She bought a bag of apples, a bunch of bananas, and a box of laundry detergent and put them inside her pants before walking out again. The two men looked at each other and raised their eyebrows. As they walked into the storeroom at the back of the store, one of them glanced down at the storekeeper's feet. He was wearing two large plastic fish.

"Unusual shoes," said the short man.

"Oh, bery comfortable," said the storekeeper. "Just righd for this hob webber."

The customs officers found nothing suspicious in the store and continued down the street.

Everyone they passed wore the same red balls on their noses and slapped along with plastic fish on their feet.

Shoppers came and went with their purchases stuffed into their extraordinarily large pants. The tall man couldn't hold back his curiosity any longer. He stopped Poppy's father and asked him why everyone was wearing red balls on their noses.

"Is it for charity?" he asked.

"Oh no," said Poppy's father, removing his nose to speak. "It's the smell of the fish. Can't stand it. None of us can."

"I can't smell any fish," said the tall man.

"Really?" said Poppy's father. "You'd better get your nose checked by the doctor!"

The tall man sniffed and looked worried.

After searching the stores, the customs officers began a house-to-house search.

They started with Poppy's house, where Poppy was outside in the yard, picking apples. She wore a red ball on her nose, of course, and a big baggy pair of pants. But she also had a giant spring attached to her feet, and she was using this to bounce up to the branches of the apple tree. At every bounce she picked an apple and stuffed it into her pants. Then she bounced again. The two men in dark suits looked at each other and, scratching their heads, walked off.

They continued their search for the stolen cargo. In one house they found a man bouncing up to the ceiling so that he could change a light bulb. Outside, a woman was cleaning the windows in the same way, wiping a patch as she reached the top of her bounce, then dipping her cloth in the pail on the ground before bouncing up again.

And everywhere they went they heard the *slap, slap, slap* of people walking along in their fish footwear.

The customs officers searched every house and every store in town, but there was no sign of stolen goods. No crates or boxes jammed into closets or under beds. Nothing.

When it was time to leave, the shorter man stopped to do some shopping. He came out with a red ball and a pair of plastic fish, size 10.

"Very reasonable price, these fish shoes," he said.

The taller man said, as they climbed back into their car, "So, no sign of contraband. They seem like pleasant people here in

Pomberton. Hard-working and honest,
I'd say. Completely mad, of course, but hard-
working and honest just the same."

"Oh, I don'd dow aboud mad," said the
shorter man, through his red nose. "These
fish shoes are really bery comferdable."

Cooking Up a Storm

I'm a wizard in the kitchen,
Or so my friends all say,
Just wait till they discover what
I'm cooking up today!

I've got my biggest caldron
Heating up on the fire,
And I've gathered the ingredients
This fine spell will require!

First a handful of cat's whiskers,
The tails from three young pups,
A big ladle full of eyeballs,
And froggy slime—two cups!

Add a ton of giant fireworks,
A bunch of old tin cans,
A pair of cymbals, a big bass drum—
All stirred with a frying pan.

Bangs and crashes shake the windows,
It's raining cats and dogs,
Outside the storm is stirring up
A nasty shower of frogs!

For, although it may be August,
So sunny, bright and warm,
You'd better run for cover—
I've cooked up the perfect storm!

King Stinky

There once lived a king who was very fond of gardening. The royal garden was the talk of the kingdom, and the king spent most of his time tending the royal blooms. They were the most magnificent flowers you could ever imagine. There were vibrant violets, delicate delphiniums, marvelous marigolds, and even lovely ruby red roses. The king could grow just about anything, and everyone said he had a green thumb, but this was largely due to the fact that he never washed his hands.

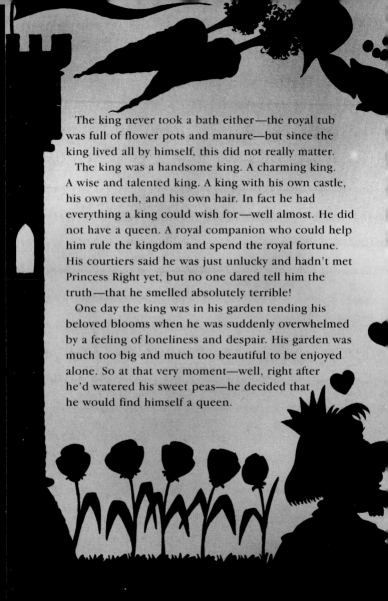

The king never took a bath either—the royal tub was full of flower pots and manure—but since the king lived all by himself, this did not really matter.

The king was a handsome king. A charming king. A wise and talented king. A king with his own castle, his own teeth, and his own hair. In fact he had everything a king could wish for—well almost. He did not have a queen. A royal companion who could help him rule the kingdom and spend the royal fortune. His courtiers said he was just unlucky and hadn't met Princess Right yet, but no one dared tell him the truth—that he smelled absolutely terrible!

One day the king was in his garden tending his beloved blooms when he was suddenly overwhelmed by a feeling of loneliness and despair. His garden was much too big and much too beautiful to be enjoyed alone. So at that very moment—well, right after he'd watered his sweet peas—he decided that he would find himself a queen.

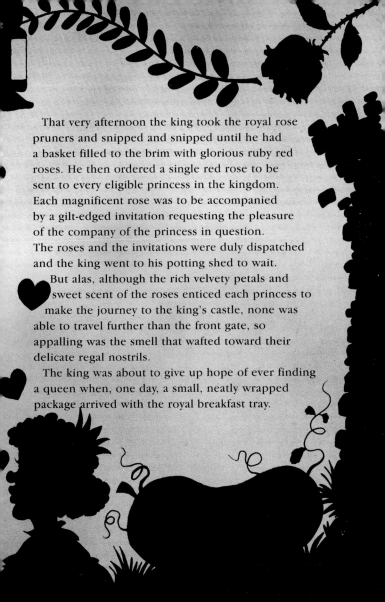

That very afternoon the king took the royal rose
pruners and snipped and snipped until he had
a basket filled to the brim with glorious ruby red
roses. He then ordered a single red rose to be
sent to every eligible princess in the kingdom.
Each magnificent rose was to be accompanied
by a gilt-edged invitation requesting the pleasure
of the company of the princess in question.
The roses and the invitations were duly dispatched
and the king went to his potting shed to wait.

But alas, although the rich velvety petals and
sweet scent of the roses enticed each princess to
make the journey to the king's castle, none was
able to travel further than the front gate, so
appalling was the smell that wafted toward their
delicate regal nostrils.

The king was about to give up hope of ever finding
a queen when, one day, a small, neatly wrapped
package arrived with the royal breakfast tray.

Inside was a tiny bottle of vibrant orange liquid and a short hand written note, which read:

Her Royal Highness regrets that she is unable to accept your invitation, but thanks you for the delightful rose, which did incidentally have a few aphids. Her Royal Highness has therefore taken the liberty of enclosing an excellent preparation which should combat this.

The king was intrigued. The very next day he ordered that one dozen royal red roses, minus aphids, of course, be dispatched directly to the princess with another invitation asking if she would join him for afternoon tea on Tuesday at four o'clock.

The next morning the king received a large, neatly wrapped package containing a splendid cabbage and a short handwritten note, which read:

Her Royal Highness thanks you most sincerely for the generous bouquet and trusts that you will accept this cabbage as a token of her appreciation. Sadly she is unable to accept your offer of tea.

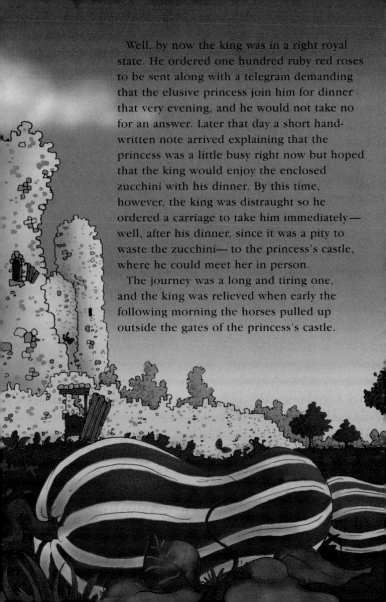

Well, by now the king was in a right royal state. He ordered one hundred ruby red roses to be sent along with a telegram demanding that the elusive princess join him for dinner that very evening, and he would not take no for an answer. Later that day a short hand-written note arrived explaining that the princess was a little busy right now but hoped that the king would enjoy the enclosed zucchini with his dinner. By this time, however, the king was distraught so he ordered a carriage to take him immediately— well, after his dinner, since it was a pity to waste the zucchini— to the princess's castle, where he could meet her in person.

The journey was a long and tiring one, and the king was relieved when early the following morning the horses pulled up outside the gates of the princess's castle.

The king clambered out and gazed at the crumbling towers that held the crumbling walls of the castle together. It was very, very run-down. The gates were rusty, and one was hanging off its hinges. Unperturbed, the king walked up the uneven, muddy driveway and knocked at the rotten front door of the castle. There was no reply, so he knocked again. He would have knocked a third time, but the knocker came off in his hand, so he decided to try the back entrance instead. He went through a rickety wooden door set in an ancient moss-covered wall and found himself in the most fantastic vegetable garden he had ever seen.

There were squashes bigger than carriages, big fat pea pods ready to burst, cabbages, cauliflowers, and lettuces all growing in perfectly straight lines and in such abundance it took your breath away.

At the far end of the garden he saw a figure effortlessly pulling up bunches of enormous juicy carrots and throwing them into the basket by her side. She was tall and very strong. Her hair was the color of the carrots and hung in unruly curls around her mud-streaked face. Her patched trousers were held up with string. She paused to wipe her nose on her sleeve and it was love at first sight. The king gave a little cough to attract her attention. The vision of loveliness looked up and the king walked steadily over to her, not noticing that she didn't smell particularly nice. He bowed politely and kissed her grimy hand.

The princess blushed the color of the wonderful beet that were sitting in her basket. "I'm so glad you came," she said, offering him a radish. "It's been lonely since the staff left."

"You're very beautiful," the king told her, and he meant it. The princess smiled a shy smile. "Oh you're just being nice," she said. "I'm afraid I've been so wrapped up in the garden that I've neglected myself."

"Nonsense," said the king. "You are by far the prettiest flower in your garden."

"You are very kind," said the princess—who was much too polite to point out that she only grew vegetables.

The king then knelt in the slimy green mud to propose. Princess Composta, for that was her name, accepted without hesitation.

"We must be married at once," announced the king, and so they were—well, after he'd helped her dig up the potatoes.

And they both lived smellily ever after.

Weird and Weirder

"Meow!"

Tommy looked up at the faint sound of a kitten purring somewhere above his head. Then he blinked in amazement. The kitten was not stuck in a tree—it appeared to be floating down through the sky! Even more incredibly, other kittens were gently falling downward. It couldn't be true! Were his eyes playing tricks? He looked up again. But it was true! And there were puppies floating down, too!

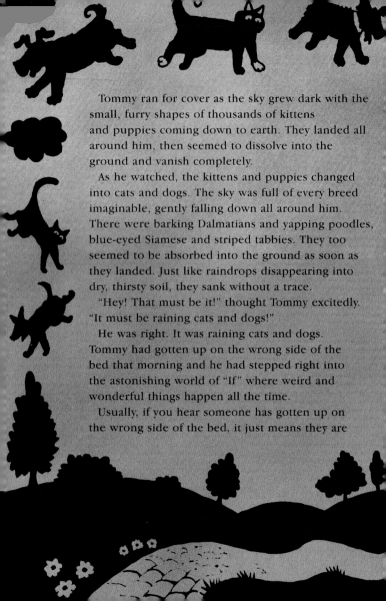

Tommy ran for cover as the sky grew dark with the small, furry shapes of thousands of kittens and puppies coming down to earth. They landed all around him, then seemed to dissolve into the ground and vanish completely.

As he watched, the kittens and puppies changed into cats and dogs. The sky was full of every breed imaginable, gently falling down all around him. There were barking Dalmatians and yapping poodles, blue-eyed Siamese and striped tabbies. They too seemed to be absorbed into the ground as soon as they landed. Just like raindrops disappearing into dry, thirsty soil, they sank without a trace.

"Hey! That must be it!" thought Tommy excitedly. "It must be raining cats and dogs!"

He was right. It was raining cats and dogs. Tommy had gotten up on the wrong side of the bed that morning and he had stepped right into the astonishing world of "If" where weird and wonderful things happen all the time.

Usually, if you hear someone has gotten up on the wrong side of the bed, it just means they are

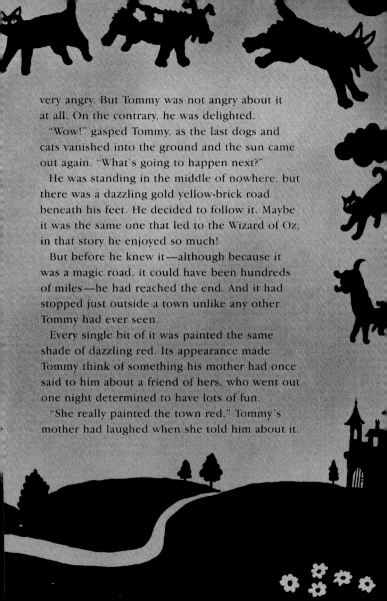

very angry. But Tommy was not angry about it at all. On the contrary, he was delighted.

"Wow!" gasped Tommy, as the last dogs and cats vanished into the ground and the sun came out again. "What's going to happen next?"

He was standing in the middle of nowhere, but there was a dazzling gold yellow-brick road beneath his feet. He decided to follow it. Maybe it was the same one that led to the Wizard of Oz, in that story he enjoyed so much!

But before he knew it—although because it was a magic road, it could have been hundreds of miles—he had reached the end. And it had stopped just outside a town unlike any other Tommy had ever seen.

Every single bit of it was painted the same shade of dazzling red. Its appearance made Tommy think of something his mother had once said to him about a friend of hers, who went out one night determined to have lots of fun.

"She really painted the town red," Tommy's mother had laughed when she told him about it.

Tommy knew that meant she'd had a really good time, not that she'd spent the whole night with a paintbrush in her hand. That wouldn't have been much fun! Looking at this town, however, it looked as if someone had done precisely that.

The fact that absolutely everything, even the trees and flowers, were the same shade of red was not the only weird thing about the town. It also seemed to be completely deserted.

Or was it? Out of the corner of his eye, Tommy thought he saw moving figures. It was very spooky.

"This looks like a ghost town," thought Tommy.

He was right. It was full of ghosts. But these ghosts were frightened of him!

"You're not going to haunt us, are you?" a friendly phantom plucked up courage to ask Tommy. "We've heard that humans go around wailing and clanking chains."

Tommy was about to reply, "No, that's what ghosts do!" but he realized that everything was backwards here. So he just smiled and said that of course he wouldn't.

However, Tommy was feeling a little nervous himself, and he wanted to explore the strange new world.

"I'm tired of seeing red," he told the phantom. "It's driving me up the wall."

His words came true. A moment later, Tommy found himself standing on top of a great wall that went all around the town.

"I've been told that walls have ears," Tommy told it, jokingly. "Maybe you do! You are totally unlike any wall I've ever met."

"You don't have to shout!" the wall retorted, proving that it did have excellent hearing.

Just then, a loud and very unexpected "Oink" sounded above Tommy's head, followed by a succession of noisy grunts. Tommy looked up and was amazed to see a herd of pigs flying toward him. They had made a V-shaped formation, like geese, but squealed rather than honked as they flew, propelling themselves along by flapping their huge pink ears.

"Well, if it can rain cats and dogs, there's no reason why pigs shouldn't fly!" Tommy laughed. "Maybe we could even hitch a ride on the back of one."

"Come on!" he shouted to the friendly ghost.

They both rose to the occasion—in the wonderful world of "If", you really can—and floated upward to join the flying pigs.

"You want to go the whole hog, do you?" squealed a large black-and-white sow with ten spotted piglets fluttering along behind her. "Well, jump aboard."

She flew them down to a beach and then took off again.

"I must keep up with the others," she grunted, "in order to save my bacon!"

Tommy and the ghost made for the inviting blue ocean. Strangely, it seemed to be singing. As Tommy got closer, he realized it was the sound of many different singsong voices, all talking at once but very softly. He couldn't hear what they were saying to him, but it all sounded very flattering.

"I think they must be whispering sweet nothings to me," Tommy laughed.

"Whhoo-oo, I love sweet nothings!" the ghost moaned with pleasure. "I'll sit here for a while and fish for compliments."

He produced a fishing net out of thin air and dipped it into the ocean. But all he got for his efforts, was a sackful of trouble.

This being "If," however, it was not an imaginary sack full of imaginary troubles, it was the real thing.

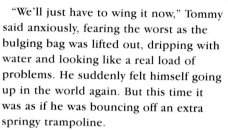

"We'll just have to wing it now," Tommy said anxiously, fearing the worst as the bulging bag was lifted out, dripping with water and looking like a real load of problems. He suddenly felt himself going up in the world again. But this time it was as if he was bouncing off an extra springy trampoline.

"We *are* winging it!" Tommy called to the phantom delightedly. "We're really flying."

But when he finally came down to earth again with a bump, there was no sign of the friendly ghost. In fact, he was right back where he had started—in bed.

And Tommy did wonder if he might not have dreamed the whole thing. Just in case, he quickly looked out the window to see if it was still raining cats and dogs— but there was only a clear blue sky!

When Dreams Come True

There's a town called Corking, not far from here,
Where dreams come true every hundred years.
"That sounds terrific," I hear you cry,
But it isn't so great, and I'll tell you why.

There was a girl named Mag with feet so large
That people cried, "They're as big as a barge!"
She wished for little feet, small and round,
But when she got them, she kept falling down.

A man named Sam wanted a sea of beer,
And that's what he got—right up to his ears.
You'd think a sea of beer would satisfy him,
But the trouble was, he couldn't swim.

There was a girl named Lucy who climbed into trees,
Because she wanted to talk to the birds and bees,
But the sparrows and starlings all wanted to chat,
And Lucy just couldn't compete with all that.

There was a boy named Arnie who wished he was strong.
His dream came true, but it didn't last long.
Everything he touched just snapped into two,
And in no time at all, he had run out of glue.

So you see what I'm getting at in this little rhyme,
You can figure it out, if you give it some time.
Beware what you wish for— and I'm talking to you—
You never know, it might come true!

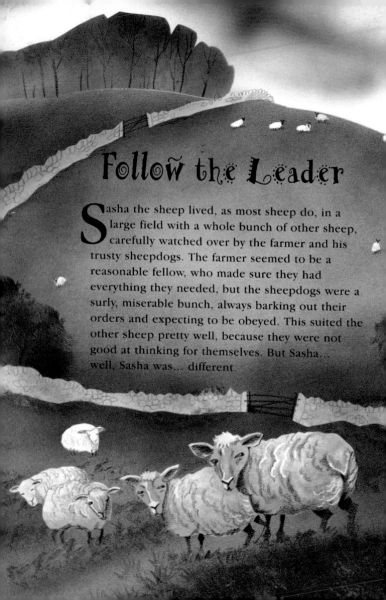

Follow the Leader

Sasha the sheep lived, as most sheep do, in a large field with a whole bunch of other sheep, carefully watched over by the farmer and his trusty sheepdogs. The farmer seemed to be a reasonable fellow, who made sure they had everything they needed, but the sheepdogs were a surly, miserable bunch, always barking out their orders and expecting to be obeyed. This suited the other sheep pretty well, because they were not good at thinking for themselves. But Sasha… well, Sasha was… different.

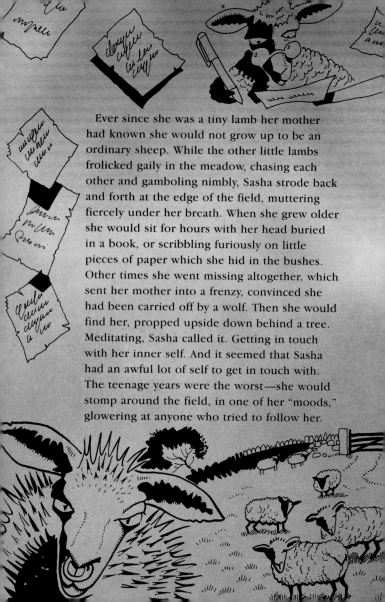

Ever since she was a tiny lamb her mother had known she would not grow up to be an ordinary sheep. While the other little lambs frolicked gaily in the meadow, chasing each other and gamboling nimbly, Sasha strode back and forth at the edge of the field, muttering fiercely under her breath. When she grew older she would sit for hours with her head buried in a book, or scribbling furiously on little pieces of paper which she hid in the bushes. Other times she went missing altogether, which sent her mother into a frenzy, convinced she had been carried off by a wolf. Then she would find her, propped upside down behind a tree. Meditating, Sasha called it. Getting in touch with her inner self. And it seemed that Sasha had an awful lot of self to get in touch with. The teenage years were the worst—she would stomp around the field, in one of her "moods," glowering at anyone who tried to follow her.

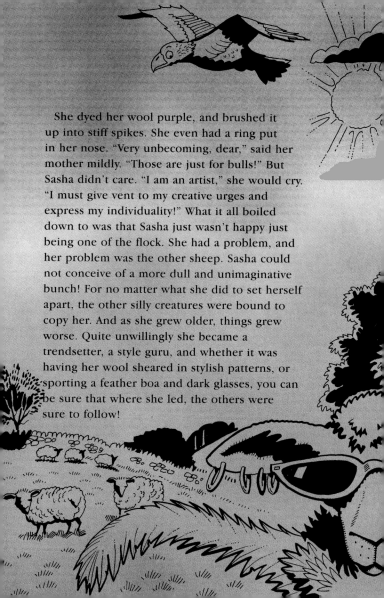

She dyed her wool purple, and brushed it up into stiff spikes. She even had a ring put in her nose. "Very unbecoming, dear," said her mother mildly. "Those are just for bulls!" But Sasha didn't care. "I am an artist," she would cry. "I must give vent to my creative urges and express my individuality!" What it all boiled down to was that Sasha just wasn't happy just being one of the flock. She had a problem, and her problem was the other sheep. Sasha could not conceive of a more dull and unimaginative bunch! For no matter what she did to set herself apart, the other silly creatures were bound to copy her. And as she grew older, things grew worse. Quite unwillingly she became a trendsetter, a style guru, and whether it was having her wool sheared in stylish patterns, or sporting a feather boa and dark glasses, you can be sure that where she led, the others were sure to follow!

"It's the highest form of flattery, dear!" said her mother. "Baloney!" said Sasha.

And so it was one morning that Sasha woke in a particularly foul temper, having discovered all the other sheep copying her latest "pirate" look —eyepatch and polka-dot bandanna—to find a handsome new sheepdog standing over her. "Get lost!" she growled, staring up at him.

"You must be Sasha," he smiled. "I've heard a lot about you from the other dogs—none of it good, I must say! I'm Sid. Do me a favor and come and lead this goofy bunch into the next field, would you? I want to make a good impression on my first day!" Now, as a rule, Sasha never did anything a dog asked her to. But there was something about Sid that made her sit up and pay attention. He was different from the others. Pleasant, for one thing. And then she noticed that his eyes were different colors—one blue, one brown!

"How wonderfully individual," thought Sasha. The fact he thought the other sheep were goofy was just the icing on the cake! Sasha was smitten! The farmer could hardly believe his eyes when he saw Sasha jump up and do exactly as Sid directed. She had always been so very difficult before. Well, well, well— perhaps she'd finally met her match!

Which, of course, is exactly what had happened, although not in the way the farmer was thinking. From then on Sasha and Sid were inseparable. In fact, the farmer was so impressed by their teamwork that he decided to enter them in the sheepdog trials at the upcoming county fair. Dutifully they practiced their routine every day, with Sid lying low in the grass listening attentively to the farmer's low whistles, and directing Sasha in a series of intricate maneuvers. They were

magnificent, moving together as one, in perfect harmony. The farmer was sure they would take the county fair by storm. Little did he know that is just what they were planning to do—but again, not in the way the farmer was thinking! For every night, once the others were asleep, Sasha and Sid had been hard at work secretly practicing a special routine of their own!

Well, the day of the sheepdog trials finally dawned, and there was great excitement as the sheepdogs rounded up the sheep and herded them, led of course by Sasha, into the farmer's truck. At the show, they sat dutifully in their pen, and watched team after team of dogs and sheep go through their maneuvers.

"Mind-numbingly dull, isn't it!" Sasha muttered to Sid. "Have they no imagination at all?"

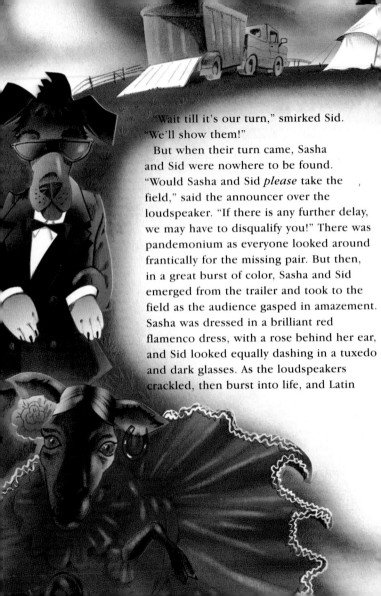

"Wait till it's our turn," smirked Sid. "We'll show them!"

But when their turn came, Sasha and Sid were nowhere to be found. "Would Sasha and Sid *please* take the field," said the announcer over the loudspeaker. "If there is any further delay, we may have to disqualify you!" There was pandemonium as everyone looked around frantically for the missing pair. But then, in a great burst of color, Sasha and Sid emerged from the trailer and took to the field as the audience gasped in amazement. Sasha was dressed in a brilliant red flamenco dress, with a rose behind her ear, and Sid looked equally dashing in a tuxedo and dark glasses. As the loudspeakers crackled, then burst into life, and Latin

music boomed across the field, Sasha
and Sid sprang into action. They danced the
samba, lambada, and salsa, moving together
in perfect harmony! The judges were
outraged and disqualified them at once.
Never had such a thing happened
at their show! But Sasha and Sid just kept
on dancing, as the crowd clapped and
cheered, putting on a show no one would
ever forget, and securing Sasha's place in
the history books as a sheep completely
unlike any other! Even the farmer was
pleased—after all, it was great publicity!

  As she snuggled down to sleep next to
Sid that night, Sasha felt truly happy. She
had made her mark at last. Interestingly
enough, though, salsa dancing has
become awfully popular these days....

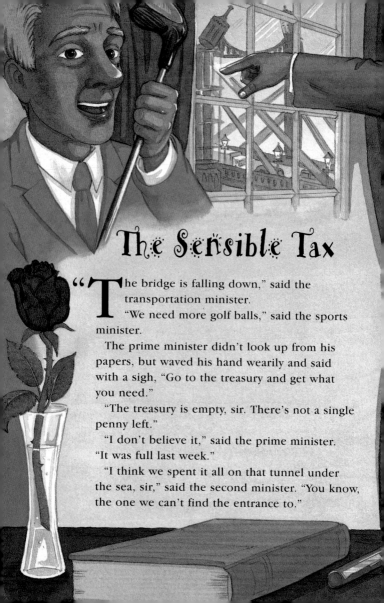

The Sensible Tax

"The bridge is falling down," said the transportation minister.

"We need more golf balls," said the sports minister.

The prime minister didn't look up from his papers, but waved his hand wearily and said with a sigh, "Go to the treasury and get what you need."

"The treasury is empty, sir. There's not a single penny left."

"I don't believe it," said the prime minister. "It was full last week."

"I think we spent it all on that tunnel under the sea, sir," said the second minister. "You know, the one we can't find the entrance to."

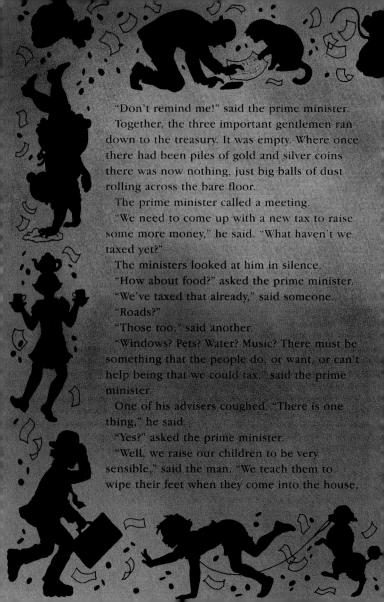

"Don't remind me!" said the prime minister.

Together, the three important gentlemen ran down to the treasury. It was empty. Where once there had been piles of gold and silver coins there was now nothing, just big balls of dust rolling across the bare floor.

The prime minister called a meeting.

"We need to come up with a new tax to raise some more money," he said. "What haven't we taxed yet?"

The ministers looked at him in silence.

"How about food?" asked the prime minister.

"We've taxed that already," said someone.

"Roads?"

"Those too," said another.

"Windows? Pets? Water? Music? There must be something that the people do, or want, or can't help being that we could tax," said the prime minister.

One of his advisers coughed. "There is one thing," he said.

"Yes?" asked the prime minister.

"Well, we raise our children to be very sensible," said the man. "We teach them to wipe their feet when they come into the house, to brush their teeth before they go to bed, not to wipe their noses on their sleeves..."

"Absolutely," interrupted the prime minister.

"...Which means that most people are sensible..."

"And we can tax them for it," said the prime minister. "That's brilliant."

So the prime minister introduced the Sensible Tax. Anyone who behaved sensibly would have to pay money to the Treasury. Tax officals were sent out to collect the money, and at first it was a great success.

They taxed people for getting to work on time, for carrying umbrellas if it looked as if it was going to rain. They taxed people for walking their dogs, for not eating snacks between meals, for taking the bus if where they were going was too far to walk.

Once the tax officials got used to the new tax, there seemed no end of things they could tax people for. At soccer games they taxed every single player for kicking the ball toward the other team's goal, at the track meets they taxed all the runners for sprinting toward the finish line. The treasury soon began to fill up again.

Of course, the new tax wasn't very popular with the people, and soon they began to grumble.

"I've just been taxed for wearing my scarf," said Benjamin's dad when he came home from work one evening.

"Why were you wearing your scarf, George?" asked his wife, Myrtle.

"Well, it's cold out," he said.

"Yes, of course," she replied.

"This is ridiculous," said George. "All our lives we are told to be sensible and now they charge us for it. It's not a sensible tax, it's a completely stupid tax. The only people who never have to pay anything are the ones who are as nutty as fruitcakes."

Just then there was a knock at the door.

"I'm a tax official," said the man at the door.

"This is just a random house check. Am I correct in thinking that you are about to eat dinner at dinnertime, ma'am?" asked the man.

"Yes," said Myrtle.

"And is it piping hot and straight from the oven?" asked the man.

"Yes," came the reply.

"And is it cooked all the way through? And will you be sitting at the dinner table to eat it, ma'am? And is there dessert to follow?"

Myrtle answered "yes" to all of these questions, and the official handed her a tax bill.

Just then Benjamin came wandering down the stairs wearing a wetsuit, a pair of flippers, and a top hat on his head.

"I don't want dinner," he said to his mom. "I've been eating chocolate all day. I'm going out now. I'll be back long after my bedtime."

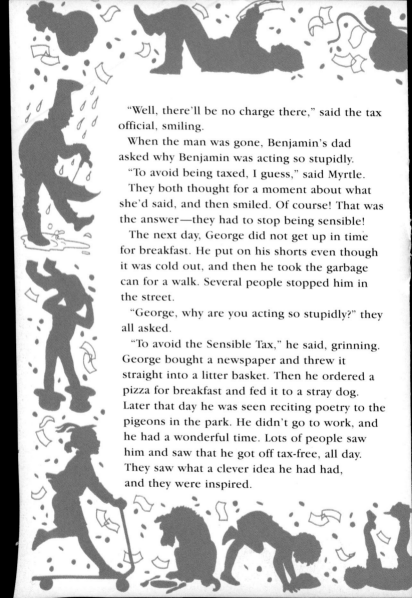

"Well, there'll be no charge there," said the tax official, smiling.

When the man was gone, Benjamin's dad asked why Benjamin was acting so stupidly.

"To avoid being taxed, I guess," said Myrtle.

They both thought for a moment about what she'd said, and then smiled. Of course! That was the answer—they had to stop being sensible!

The next day, George did not get up in time for breakfast. He put on his shorts even though it was cold out, and then he took the garbage can for a walk. Several people stopped him in the street.

"George, why are you acting so stupidly?" they all asked.

"To avoid the Sensible Tax," he said, grinning. George bought a newspaper and threw it straight into a litter basket. Then he ordered a pizza for breakfast and fed it to a stray dog. Later that day he was seen reciting poetry to the pigeons in the park. He didn't go to work, and he had a wonderful time. Lots of people saw him and saw that he got off tax-free, all day. They saw what a clever idea he had had, and they were inspired.

The next day, most people didn't go to work at all, and those who did didn't get there on time; some even went to the wrong jobs. They walked if it was too far to walk; if they had bicycles, they carried them. A lot of people went to the movies in the afternoon dressed as pirates, but they didn't watch the film. No, that would have been too sensible. Instead, they faced the back of the theater and sang silly songs at the tops of their voices.

They all had a great day, and the next day they all got up late and did it all over again, only this time they found even more ways to be silly.

The tax officials began to get worried— the money had stopped coming in—and the government ministers were even more worried. No one was doing any work; the country was falling apart. They called an emergency meeting with the prime minister.

"Sorry I'm late," said the prime minister. "My train didn't leave on time, and then it went off in the wrong direction. It's chaos out there. What's going on?"

"It's the Sensible Tax, sir," said one of his ministers. "Everyone is acting stupidly so that they don't have to pay it."

"Well, this can't go on," said the prime minister. "The country's gone mad."

"We'll have to cancel the tax," someone said.

The prime minister paused. He liked the Sensible Tax; it raised lots of money. Without it the treasury would be empty again. But things were getting out of hand.

"Yes," he said sadly. And then he smiled. "I've got it," he cried. "Why don't we tax people for wearing clothes?"

All the ministers threw up their hands in complete despair.

"Oh no!" they groaned.

It's Raining

It's raining cats and dogs,
  And warty toads and frogs,
  And red-kneed bats and derby hats.
It's raining big fat hogs.

It's raining needles and pins,
And rusty cans and tins,
And things I don't like— such as pieces of bike.
It's raining old clothes pins.

It's raining sugar and spice,
And sleek white rats and mice,
And currant buns and somebody's sons.
It's raining furry dice.

It's raining apples and pears,
And dolls and teddy bears,
And silly pigs in curly wigs.
It's raining plastic chairs.

It's raining smelly socks,
And pebbles, stones, and rocks,
And grease-stained ties and old pot pies.
It's raining party frocks.

It's raining tropical fruits,
And cowboy hats and suits.
And hairy legs and bacon and eggs.
It's raining shoes and boots.

It's raining ducks and drakes,
And chocolate bars and cakes,
And glasses of milk and colorful silk.
It's raining garden rakes.

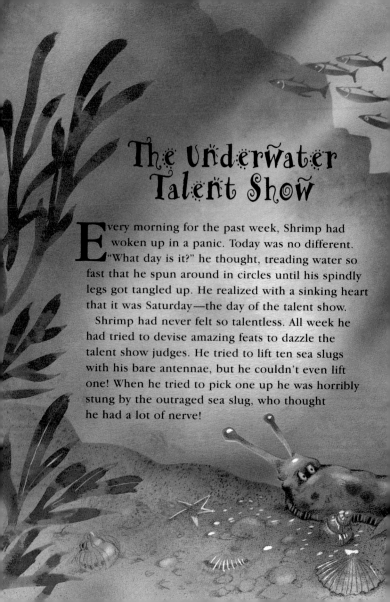

The Underwater Talent Show

Every morning for the past week, Shrimp had woken up in a panic. Today was no different. "What day is it?" he thought, treading water so fast that he spun around in circles until his spindly legs got tangled up. He realized with a sinking heart that it was Saturday—the day of the talent show.

Shrimp had never felt so talentless. All week he had tried to devise amazing feats to dazzle the talent show judges. He tried to lift ten sea slugs with his bare antennae, but he couldn't even lift one! When he tried to pick one up he was horribly stung by the outraged sea slug, who thought he had a lot of nerve!

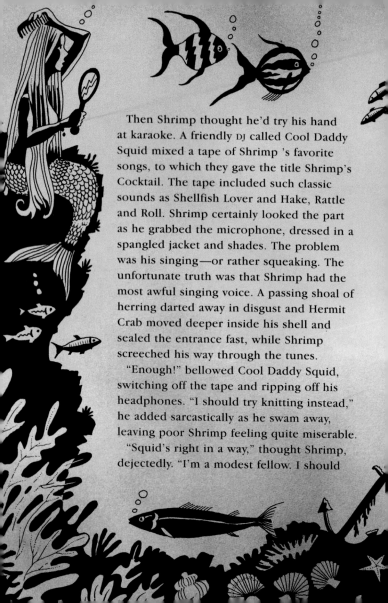

Then Shrimp thought he'd try his hand at karaoke. A friendly DJ called Cool Daddy Squid mixed a tape of Shrimp 's favorite songs, to which they gave the title Shrimp's Cocktail. The tape included such classic sounds as Shellfish Lover and Hake, Rattle and Roll. Shrimp certainly looked the part as he grabbed the microphone, dressed in a spangled jacket and shades. The problem was his singing—or rather squeaking. The unfortunate truth was that Shrimp had the most awful singing voice. A passing shoal of herring darted away in disgust and Hermit Crab moved deeper inside his shell and sealed the entrance fast, while Shrimp screeched his way through the tunes.

"Enough!" bellowed Cool Daddy Squid, switching off the tape and ripping off his headphones. "I should try knitting instead," he added sarcastically as he swam away, leaving poor Shrimp feeling quite miserable.

"Squid's right in a way," thought Shrimp, dejectedly. "I'm a modest fellow. I should

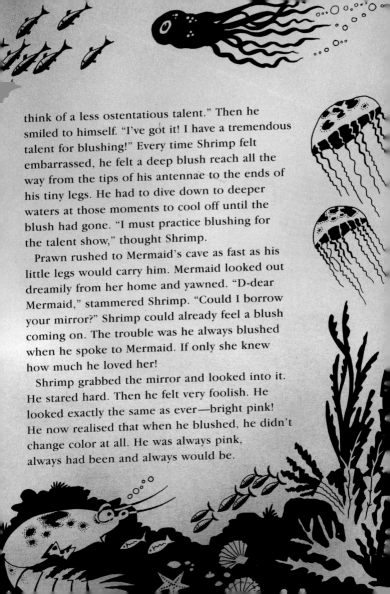

think of a less ostentatious talent." Then he smiled to himself. "I've got it! I have a tremendous talent for blushing!" Every time Shrimp felt embarrassed, he felt a deep blush reach all the way from the tips of his antennae to the ends of his tiny legs. He had to dive down to deeper waters at those moments to cool off until the blush had gone. "I must practice blushing for the talent show," thought Shrimp.

Prawn rushed to Mermaid's cave as fast as his little legs would carry him. Mermaid looked out dreamily from her home and yawned. "D-dear Mermaid," stammered Shrimp. "Could I borrow your mirror?" Shrimp could already feel a blush coming on. The trouble was he always blushed when he spoke to Mermaid. If only she knew how much he loved her!

Shrimp grabbed the mirror and looked into it. He stared hard. Then he felt very foolish. He looked exactly the same as ever—bright pink! He now realised that when he blushed, he didn't change color at all. He was always pink, always had been and always would be.

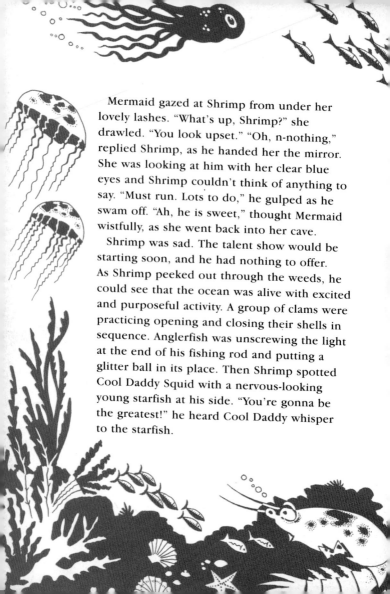

Mermaid gazed at Shrimp from under her lovely lashes. "What's up, Shrimp?" she drawled. "You look upset." "Oh, n-nothing," replied Shrimp, as he handed her the mirror. She was looking at him with her clear blue eyes and Shrimp couldn't think of anything to say. "Must run. Lots to do," he gulped as he swam off. "Ah, he is sweet," thought Mermaid wistfully, as she went back into her cave.

Shrimp was sad. The talent show would be starting soon, and he had nothing to offer. As Shrimp peeked out through the weeds, he could see that the ocean was alive with excited and purposeful activity. A group of clams were practicing opening and closing their shells in sequence. Anglerfish was unscrewing the light at the end of his fishing rod and putting a glitter ball in its place. Then Shrimp spotted Cool Daddy Squid with a nervous-looking young starfish at his side. "You're gonna be the greatest!" he heard Cool Daddy whisper to the starfish.

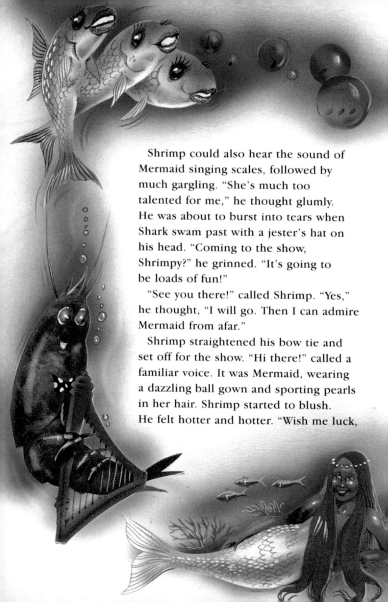

Shrimp could also hear the sound of
Mermaid singing scales, followed by
much gargling. "She's much too
talented for me," he thought glumly.
He was about to burst into tears when
Shark swam past with a jester's hat on
his head. "Coming to the show,
Shrimpy?" he grinned. "It's going to
be loads of fun!"

"See you there!" called Shrimp. "Yes,"
he thought, "I will go. Then I can admire
Mermaid from afar."

Shrimp straightened his bow tie and
set off for the show. "Hi there!" called a
familiar voice. It was Mermaid, wearing
a dazzling ball gown and sporting pearls
in her hair. Shrimp started to blush.
He felt hotter and hotter. "Wish me luck,

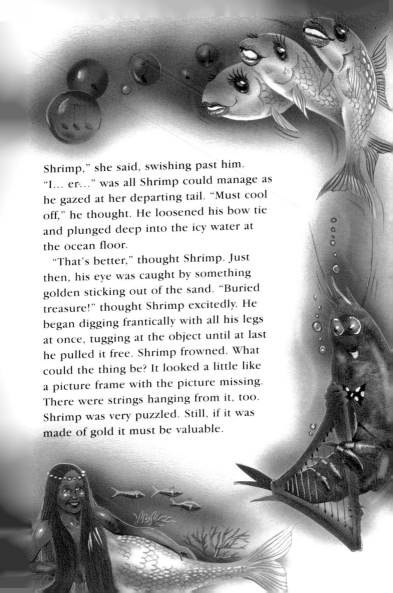

Shrimp," she said, swishing past him.
"I... er..." was all Shrimp could manage as
he gazed at her departing tail. "Must cool
off," he thought. He loosened his bow tie
and plunged deep into the icy water at
the ocean floor.

"That's better," thought Shrimp. Just
then, his eye was caught by something
golden sticking out of the sand. "Buried
treasure!" thought Shrimp excitedly. He
began digging frantically with all his legs
at once, tugging at the object until at last
he pulled it free. Shrimp frowned. What
could the thing be? It looked a little like
a picture frame with the picture missing.
There were strings hanging from it, too.
Shrimp was very puzzled. Still, if it was
made of gold it must be valuable.

Then Shrimp had a wonderful idea. He could take the thing to the talent show and auction it. Who knows, maybe he had a talent for auctioneering! He had his bow tie on. Didn't auctioneers wear bow ties? He must be made for the job! Feeling very pleased with himself, Shrimp dragged his treasure all the way to the talent show.

The show had already started when Shrimp arrived, so he slipped in at the back to watch. Octopus was on stage. He was wearing cleats on each of his eight feet and giving a fine demonstration of soccer skills. He dribbled the ball, passed it from foot to foot, and took an occasional header. The audience loved it. Then he started tap dancing, clattering out a complicated rhythm with all eight cleats. The crowd roared. Octopus took a deep bow and left the stage.

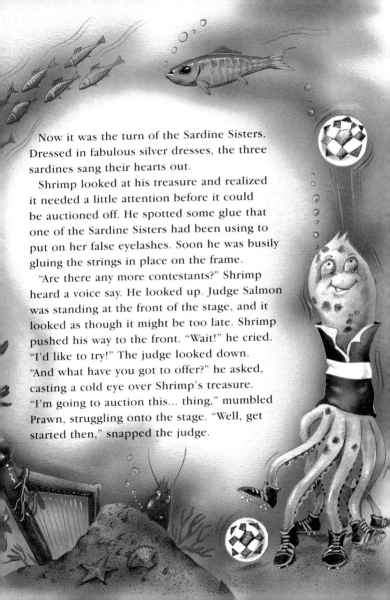

Now it was the turn of the Sardine Sisters. Dressed in fabulous silver dresses, the three sardines sang their hearts out.

Shrimp looked at his treasure and realized it needed a little attention before it could be auctioned off. He spotted some glue that one of the Sardine Sisters had been using to put on her false eyelashes. Soon he was busily gluing the strings in place on the frame.

"Are there any more contestants?" Shrimp heard a voice say. He looked up. Judge Salmon was standing at the front of the stage, and it looked as though it might be too late. Shrimp pushed his way to the front. "Wait!" he cried. "I'd like to try!" The judge looked down. "And what have you got to offer?" he asked, casting a cold eye over Shrimp's treasure. "I'm going to auction this... thing," mumbled Prawn, struggling onto the stage. "Well, get started then," snapped the judge.

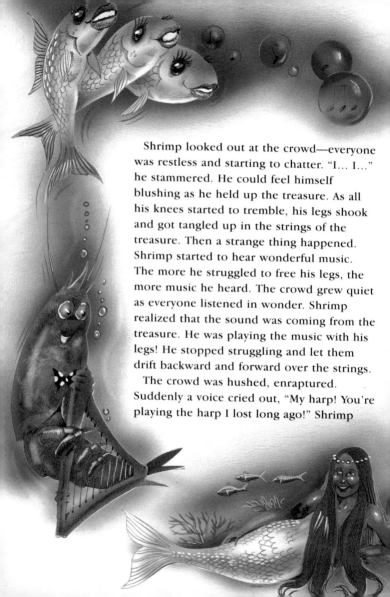

Shrimp looked out at the crowd—everyone was restless and starting to chatter. "I... I..." he stammered. He could feel himself blushing as he held up the treasure. As all his knees started to tremble, his legs shook and got tangled up in the strings of the treasure. Then a strange thing happened. Shrimp started to hear wonderful music. The more he struggled to free his legs, the more music he heard. The crowd grew quiet as everyone listened in wonder. Shrimp realized that the sound was coming from the treasure. He was playing the music with his legs! He stopped struggling and let them drift backward and forward over the strings.

The crowd was hushed, enraptured. Suddenly a voice cried out, "My harp! You're playing the harp I lost long ago!" Shrimp

looked up. Mermaid was swimming
toward him with tears in her eyes. She
rushed up onto the stage and kissed and
hugged him joyfully. "Thank you,
Shrimp!" she cried. "You have played the
most beautiful music on my harp that I
have ever heard." The crowd cheered.
Shrimp blushed.

"I suppose you could call it a hidden
talent," he said.

The Planet Where Time Goes Backwards

Far beyond our solar system,
In the outer reaches of space,
There's a planet where time goes backwards,
And it's the most peculiar place.

A place where birds climb into their shells,
And leaves flutter up to the trees,
Clouds suck rain from out of the ground,
And rivers flow out of the seas.

Cooks wash the dishes before the meal starts
And unpeel potatoes, I'm told.
Your dinner goes into the oven,
And comes out nice and cold.

Construction workers start with a house
And take it apart brick by brick.
At lunchtime they spit out their sandwiches.
(It looks like they're being sick!)

At gas pumps they take the fuel out of cars,
And football's not much of a laugh:
The game ends with both teams at zero,
And they start by taking a bath.

You know something bad's going to happen,
When somebody starts to cry.
But the people get younger each day,
And they greet you by saying "Goodbye."

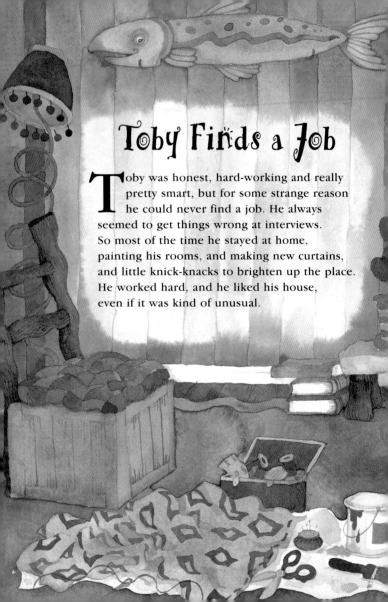

Toby Finds a Job

Toby was honest, hard-working and really pretty smart, but for some strange reason he could never find a job. He always seemed to get things wrong at interviews. So most of the time he stayed at home, painting his rooms, and making new curtains, and little knick-knacks to brighten up the place. He worked hard, and he liked his house, even if it was kind of unusual.

Toby's friends all knew that Toby was looking for a job and they were always on the lookout for things he could do. One day, his friend Suzie called to say that the office where she worked was looking for a "spokesperson".

"A 'spokesperson,'" thought Toby. "It's an unusual job, but I think I can do it." He went to his garage and took the wheels off his bicycle. Then he went to all his friends and borrowed their bicycle wheels, too. By lunchtime he had lots of wheels and hundreds of spokes. He went to the company and said:

"I'm very good with spokes! See? I've got long ones, short ones, bent ones, but most of them are straight."

The interviewer scratched his head and laughed. "No, a 'spokesperson' is someone who talks to people—newspapers, radio, and television. They tell them what the company does. It's got nothing to do with bicycle wheels."

"Oh," said Toby, and he went home again and made a new coffee table out of a big drainpipe.

The next day, Toby's friend Sam came by to say that the school down the block was looking for

someone to help out. "The person they need,"
he said, "has to be good with children." But Toby
didn't hear him right. He thought that Sam had
said "chickens".

"Chickens?" thought Toby. "In a school? That's
very unusual, but maybe they're learning about
farms, or they have a pet corner."

So he went to a nearby chicken farm and
borrowed as many chickens as he could fit into
his car. Then he went to the school.

"I'm here about the job," said Toby, unloading
the chickens. The chickens ran all over the
classroom, squawking and clucking. Feathers
flew everywhere, and the children screamed and
huddled into a corner.

"Get those chickens out of here," said the
teacher angrily.

It took Toby a long time to round up the
chickens, and by that time the teacher looked so
angry that Toby thought he'd better not ask for
a job. He went home and painted his kitchen
yellow with green polka dots.

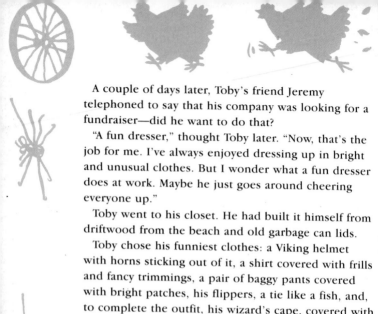

A couple of days later, Toby's friend Jeremy telephoned to say that his company was looking for a fundraiser—did he want to do that?

"A fun dresser," thought Toby later. "Now, that's the job for me. I've always enjoyed dressing up in bright and unusual clothes. But I wonder what a fun dresser does at work. Maybe he just goes around cheering everyone up."

Toby went to his closet. He had built it himself from driftwood from the beach and old garbage can lids.

Toby chose his funniest clothes: a Viking helmet with horns sticking out of it, a shirt covered with frills and fancy trimmings, a pair of baggy pants covered with bright patches, his flippers, a tie like a fish, and, to complete the outfit, his wizard's cape, covered with stars and signs of the zodiac. He wasn't sure if other people would think the cape was a fun thing to wear or not—it was the kind of thing he wore all the time.

When Toby got to the interview he leaped into the room with a loud, "Ta-daaa," and was greeted by stunned silence. The people in the office were very nicely dressed in white shirts and gray suits, and they just sat there with their mouths open.

"Isn't this fun enough?" asked Toby, surprised by their silence.

"I beg your pardon," said a stiff-looking lady with a notepad.

"Is this the kind of fun dressing you had in mind?" asked Toby. "I've got more like this at home."

The ladies and gentlemen in suits looked at each other with puzzled expressions, and then one of them laughed. Then they all laughed.

"No," one of them said at last, gulping for air. "We're looking for a 'fundraiser.' You know, someone who raises money."

"Oh," said Toby, feeling very foolish. "Not someone who dresses in funny clothes?"

"Not really," said the man, laughing so much his sides hurt.

Toby took the bus home, trying not to worry about the funny looks he was getting from the other passengers.

A few days later, all of Toby's friends came to visit him. Sam was there, and Suzie and Jeremy.

They were worried about Toby. Would he ever
find a job? Toby was excited to have all his
friends there.

"You sit there, Suzie," he said. "It's my new
inflatable chair. I made it myself out of car inner-
tubes."

"Wow! It's great!" laughed Suzie. "It really is
very comfortable."

"This chair is good, too," said Jeremy, sitting on
one Toby had made out of old packing crates.

The friends chatted and laughed. They loved
Toby, but they thought his job-hunting mistakes
were really funny.

"What about that time you went for a job as a
bookkeeper," laughed Suzie, "with all those
books under your arm."

"Well, I've got lots of books," said Toby,
bashfully. "I'm very good at keeping them."

"Yes, but a bookkeeper takes care of money,
not books," said Suzie.

"I know that now," said Toby.

"And that time you went for a job as a fencer," laughed Jeremy. "They meant putting up fences, not sword-fighting."

Toby blushed a bright pink color.

When they had stopped laughing, the friends looked around Toby's room. The walls were painted in stripes of purple and green, and the curtains were orange with little pink birds stitched onto them. It was a very unusual home, but they liked it. It was different, and it made their homes seem dull.

"Could you make me some curtains like that?" said Suzie.

Toby looked at her with surprise. No one had ever asked him to do anything like that before. "Of course," he said. "I'd like to make you some red ones with little blue boats on them."

"And can you make me a clothes closet

out of driftwood, just like yours?" asked Jeremy. "I think it's great."

Toby said he would, and the next day he got to work making Jeremy a clothes closet that was even more mixed up than his own. Jeremy loved it. Then he made Suzie the curtains she'd asked for, and then one of Suzie's friends came over wanting to buy a blow-up chair like the one Toby had made for himself.

Soon Toby was busier than he'd ever been, making strange furniture for all kinds of people and visiting their houses to paint the walls bright colors and put up his crazy curtains. And the best part was, people paid him to do it. Toby became famous. He traveled all over the world, making things for rock bands and movie stars. Toby had found a job after all, without even looking, doing what he did best.

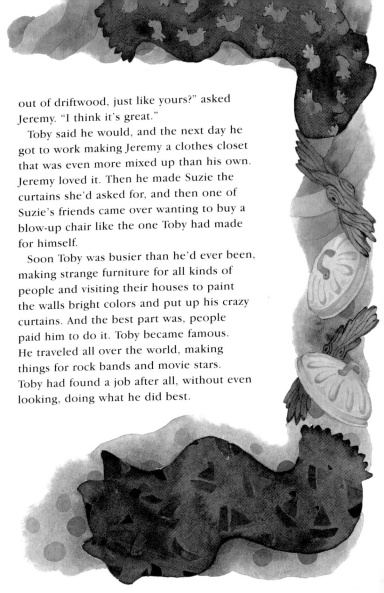

A Knight to Remembe

Long, long ago, when kings ruled over kingdoms,
fearsome dragons terrorized the lands, and
beautiful princesses swooned over dashing
knights in shining armor, there lived a very
worried man called Alfred Ramsbottom.

Alfred was a great big bear of a man, with an
important job working as chief blacksmith to the
king. He shod the king's horses, and equipped his
knights with swords, shields, and suits of armor.

Business had been very good recently because the kingdom where Alfred lived was being menaced by a large and loathsome dragon, who had gotten rid of every valiant knight that had set out to slay him. Alfred could barely keep up with the workload, as knight after knight prepared to be sent into battle. Things were so bad that the king had to put up a banner on the castle walls, which read:

Knights wanted. Must be brave, dashing, and fearless. Experience in dragon-slaying an advantage. Competitive salary, plus the hand of the princess upon defeat of the dragon.

All eligible young men should apply to the castle at the earliest opportunity.

But there had only been three applicants. They had all made very tasty breakfasts for the dragon, who was looking forward to more.

So, you are probably wondering, just what was worrying Alfred? Was it the heavy workload?

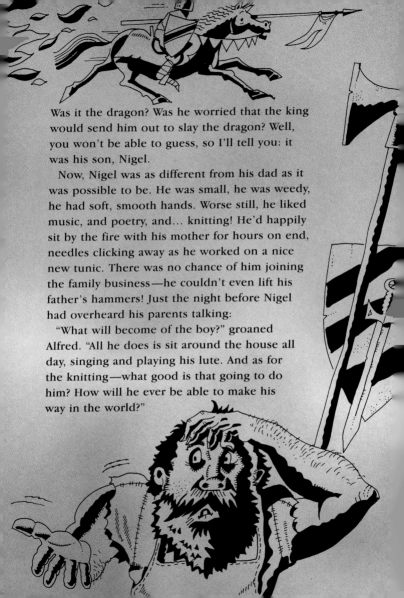

Was it the dragon? Was he worried that the king would send him out to slay the dragon? Well, you won't be able to guess, so I'll tell you: it was his son, Nigel.

Now, Nigel was as different from his dad as it was possible to be. He was small, he was weedy, he had soft, smooth hands. Worse still, he liked music, and poetry, and… knitting! He'd happily sit by the fire with his mother for hours on end, needles clicking away as he worked on a nice new tunic. There was no chance of him joining the family business—he couldn't even lift his father's hammers! Just the night before Nigel had overheard his parents talking:

"What will become of the boy?" groaned Alfred. "All he does is sit around the house all day, singing and playing his lute. And as for the knitting—what good is that going to do him? How will he ever be able to make his way in the world?"

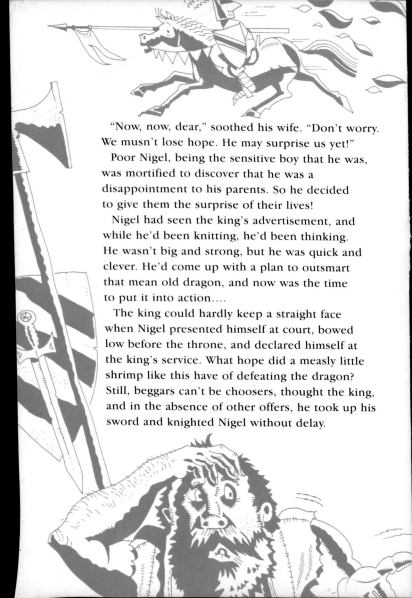

"Now, now, dear," soothed his wife. "Don't worry. We musn't lose hope. He may surprise us yet!"

Poor Nigel, being the sensitive boy that he was, was mortified to discover that he was a disappointment to his parents. So he decided to give them the surprise of their lives!

Nigel had seen the king's advertisement, and while he'd been knitting, he'd been thinking. He wasn't big and strong, but he was quick and clever. He'd come up with a plan to outsmart that mean old dragon, and now was the time to put it into action....

The king could hardly keep a straight face when Nigel presented himself at court, bowed low before the throne, and declared himself at the king's service. What hope did a measly little shrimp like this have of defeating the dragon? Still, beggars can't be choosers, thought the king, and in the absence of other offers, he took up his sword and knighted Nigel without delay.

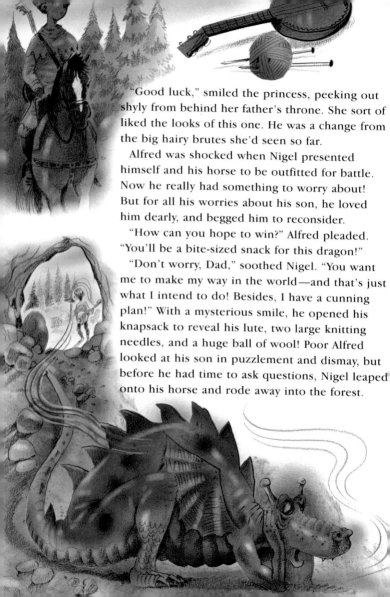

"Good luck," smiled the princess, peeking out shyly from behind her father's throne. She sort of liked the looks of this one. He was a change from the big hairy brutes she'd seen so far.

Alfred was shocked when Nigel presented himself and his horse to be outfitted for battle. Now he really had something to worry about! But for all his worries about his son, he loved him dearly, and begged him to reconsider.

"How can you hope to win?" Alfred pleaded. "You'll be a bite-sized snack for this dragon!"

"Don't worry, Dad," soothed Nigel. "You want me to make my way in the world—and that's just what I intend to do! Besides, I have a cunning plan!" With a mysterious smile, he opened his knapsack to reveal his lute, two large knitting needles, and a huge ball of wool! Poor Alfred looked at his son in puzzlement and dismay, but before he had time to ask questions, Nigel leaped onto his horse and rode away into the forest.

For four long days and nights nothing
more was heard of him.

While his parents sat anxiously at home,
Nigel was very busy. When he arrived at the
dragon's lair, he hid himself in a small crack in
the rock at the mouth of the dragon's cave. He
waited till he heard the dragon snoring away
deep in the depths, then took out his knitting
needles and the huge ball of wool. His needles
flashed as he worked furiously, and in no time
at all he had knitted a gigantic net that
stretched across the entire mouth of the cave.
Then he took out his lute and, perching high
on a rock above the cave, he began to play
the sweetest song he knew.

Now, not many people know this, but dragons
can't stand music or poetry. It jangles their
nerves, and their skin crawls and their teeth
grind. But Nigel knew, so it was no surprise to
him that his plan worked like a dream.

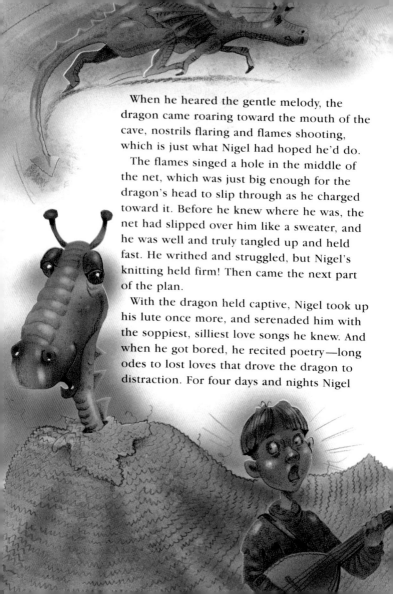

When he heared the gentle melody, the dragon came roaring toward the mouth of the cave, nostrils flaring and flames shooting, which is just what Nigel had hoped he'd do.

The flames singed a hole in the middle of the net, which was just big enough for the dragon's head to slip through as he charged toward it. Before he knew where he was, the net had slipped over him like a sweater, and he was well and truly tangled up and held fast. He writhed and struggled, but Nigel's knitting held firm! Then came the next part of the plan.

With the dragon held captive, Nigel took up his lute once more, and serenaded him with the soppiest, silliest love songs he knew. And when he got bored, he recited poetry—long odes to lost loves that drove the dragon to distraction. For four days and nights Nigel

kept up his performance, until the demented dragon could stand it no more, and begged Nigel to let him flee the kingdom to escape. Nigel kept on singing while he cut through the net, and the last time he saw the dragon, he was tearing across the distant hills, howling and holding his ears.

Nigel rode home triumphantly, and as you can imagine, the king was delighted. So was the princess, who whisked him up the aisle as fast as you can say knit one, purl one. As for Alfred, well, his worries were over at last. Nigel had made his mark as a knight to remember, and in the process had landed himself the perfect position in life, as a prince with nothing better to do than to spend his days singing, playing his lute, and knitting. And the princess never wanted for lovely sweaters. Perfect!

A Whale of a Time

Did you hear the story
Of Wendy Bligh,
The remarkable whale
Who loved to fly?

It happened like this:
She was sleeping one day
When a hot-air balloonist
Flew her way.

He looked down below
And spotted her hump,
"I'll land on that rock,"
Said he, with a thump.

He tied up his balloon
With a beautiful bow,
While Wendy slept on—
She just didn't know.

Then a big tornado
Whirled over the sea.
It blew Wendy upwards
As high as could be.

"What a wonderful feeling!"
The whale cried in glee.
"I am floating above
The sparkling blue sea."

The hot-air balloonist
Took her for a spin.
She chatted to sea birds
And waved her huge fin.

He dropped her back home
At the end of the day.
"Oh, thank you!" she smiled,
And then swam away.

Good Homes Wanted

"**M**eow, meow!" A large black-and-white cat sat on the fence outside number three Cherry Tree Avenue, watching and waiting. At exactly four o'clock a schoolboy appeared on the corner of the road and the cat arched its back and purred excitedly as its friend approached.

"Hello, cat," said the boy, whose name was Danny. "Been waiting long?"

"Meow, meow," replied the cat, which meant "Since ten-thirty this morning."

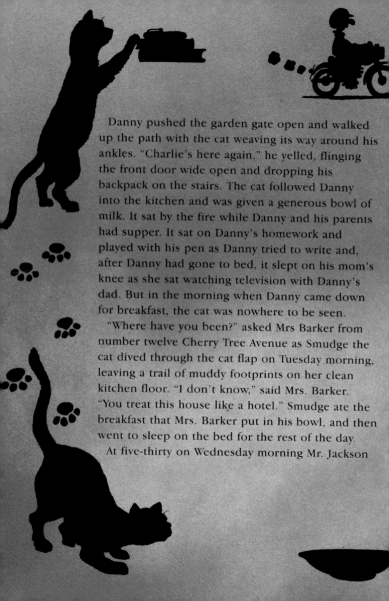

Danny pushed the garden gate open and walked up the path with the cat weaving its way around his ankles. "Charlie's here again," he yelled, flinging the front door wide open and dropping his backpack on the stairs. The cat followed Danny into the kitchen and was given a generous bowl of milk. It sat by the fire while Danny and his parents had supper. It sat on Danny's homework and played with his pen as Danny tried to write and, after Danny had gone to bed, it slept on his mom's knee as she sat watching television with Danny's dad. But in the morning when Danny came down for breakfast, the cat was nowhere to be seen.

"Where have you been?" asked Mrs Barker from number twelve Cherry Tree Avenue as Smudge the cat dived through the cat flap on Tuesday morning, leaving a trail of muddy footprints on her clean kitchen floor. "I don't know," said Mrs. Barker. "You treat this house like a hotel." Smudge ate the breakfast that Mrs. Barker put in his bowl, and then went to sleep on the bed for the rest of the day.

At five-thirty on Wednesday morning Mr. Jackson

of number twenty-six Cherry Tree Avenue was woken
by a scratch, scratch, scratching at his bedroom
window. There, smiling from whisker to whisker, was
his cat Rascal, whom he had not seen for a few days.
Mr. Jackson opened the window to let Rascal in.
"Cats!" he said, but he was actually pleased that his
furry friend had paid him another early-morning
visit. He fell back into bed, and Rascal curled up
next to him, purring very, very loudly.

At school later that same day, Danny's teacher
was asking the children who had pets to talk to
the rest of the class about them.

"I've almost got a cat," Danny told his class, which
made them all laugh. So Danny explained how the
mysterious Charlie only lived at his house on
Mondays, and occasionally on Fridays, but in
between he just disappeared completely.

"It's here again," called Mr Williams from number
thirty-five Cherry Tree Avenue, as the large cat sat on
the doorstep on Thursday morning, waiting to be
let in. Two little girls ran excitedly down the hall
toward the front door.

"Oh please let him in, Daddy," cried Suzy, the older of the two girls.

"I want to hold him," said Jenny, pushing her sister aside. Mr Williams tucked his morning paper under one arm. "Now girls, no squabbling, or you'll frighten it," he said. But there was not much chance of that. Mr. Williams opened the door just a little and the cat rushed in, rolling around on the floor enjoying the little girls' attention.

"Can we keep him?" asked Suzy.

"He could sleep on my bed," suggested Jenny helpfully.

"No, mine," insisted Suzy, and another argument broke out.

"Girls, girls," said Mrs Williams, appearing at the top of the stairs in her bathrobe. "Oh, look," she beamed as she spotted the cat. "He's come back. Do you think he'd like some bacon?" The cat rolled onto its back and pedaled an imaginary bicycle, which meant,

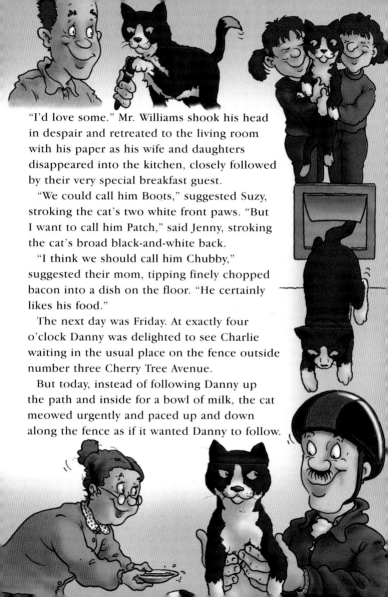

"I'd love some." Mr. Williams shook his head in despair and retreated to the living room with his paper as his wife and daughters disappeared into the kitchen, closely followed by their very special breakfast guest.

"We could call him Boots," suggested Suzy, stroking the cat's two white front paws. "But I want to call him Patch," said Jenny, stroking the cat's broad black-and-white back.

"I think we should call him Chubby," suggested their mom, tipping finely chopped bacon into a dish on the floor. "He certainly likes his food."

The next day was Friday. At exactly four o'clock Danny was delighted to see Charlie waiting in the usual place on the fence outside number three Cherry Tree Avenue.

But today, instead of following Danny up the path and inside for a bowl of milk, the cat meowed urgently and paced up and down along the fence as if it wanted Danny to follow.

"What is it?" asked Danny as the cat trotted up the street with its tail held high.

Mrs Barker was watering her hanging baskets when Smudge appeared on the doorstep with a somewhat scruffy schoolboy close behind.

"What do you want?" asked Mrs. Barker, as the cat clawed at her wrinkled stockings, making them even more wrinkled.

"He wants you to follow us," explained Danny.

"Oh, does she?" asked Mrs. Barker, looking at the boy suspiciously. Nevertheless, she put down her watering can and followed.

Soon they reached number twenty six Cherry Tree Avenue. Mr. Jackson had just gotten home from work and was climbing off his motorcycle. "Rascal, what's the matter?" he cried, as the cat clawed at his leg and then started to run off down the street.

"We must follow the cat!" said Mrs. Barker, breathlessly, as she caught up with Smudge. Mr. Jackson put his helmet back on and started his motorcycle again.

He wobbled off after Rascal, with Danny and Mrs. Barker trying desperately to keep up.

"Nyawww," went the bike as it turned the corner into Market Street. "Meow, meow," said the cat as it spotted Mr. Roe the fishseller.

"Well, I never," said Mr. Roe in surprise when he saw the strange line of people trying to keep up with a cat. Curiosity got the better of him, and he thought he had better join them—he might be missing out on something!

The cat then ran through the outdoor market closely followed by Mr. Jackson and Mr. Roe with Danny and poor old Mrs. Barker bringing up the rear.

People gazed in amazement as the cat and its pursuers disappeared around the corner into the playground.

Mrs. Williams was pushing her two daughters on the swings.

"Look, it's Socks!" cried Suzy.

"No, it's Patch," corrected Jenny, and they both jumped off the swings and followed Mr. Jackson, Mr. Roe, Danny and Mrs. Barker, whose stockings were now very, *very* wrinkled!

At last, and much to everyone's relief, the cat stopped. They all looked at each other, feeling slightly awkward and embarrassed, and then they all looked down at the cat. She seemed to be smiling as with her nose she gently made a gap in the hedge to reveal six beautiful black-and-white kittens. Kittens all ready and waiting for their new owners to take them to their purrrrrfect new homes.

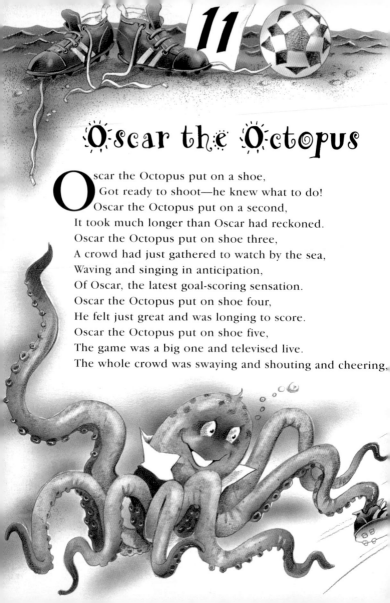

Oscar the Octopus

Oscar the Octopus put on a shoe,
Got ready to shoot—he knew what to do!
Oscar the Octopus put on a second,
It took much longer than Oscar had reckoned.
Oscar the Octopus put on shoe three,
A crowd had just gathered to watch by the sea,
Waving and singing in anticipation,
Of Oscar, the latest goal-scoring sensation.
Oscar the Octopus put on shoe four,
He felt just great and was longing to score.
Oscar the Octopus put on shoe five,
The game was a big one and televised live.
The whole crowd was swaying and shouting and cheering,

And hoping that Oscar would soon be appearing.
Oscar the Octopus put on shoe six,
And stood on his head as he practiced some kicks.
Oscar the Octopus put on shoe seven,
And straightened his jersey—he was number eleven.
He gazed in the mirror and felt really proud,
It was time for his debut in front of the crowd.
Just one more shoe—would he ever be ready?
The laces were tangled, his nerves were unsteady.
Oscar the Octopus put on shoe eight,
Walked onto the field but the Ref said, "Too late.
The game is all over, the whistle has blown,
Nobody scored, and the crowd has gone home."

Steve and Stella

"**G**ive that present to me!" Steve shouted at his sister Stella. "It's much better than mine!" He launched himself angrily at her and made a grab for the model dinosaur she had just been given by Santa Claus, who was sitting in the Christmas display of a big department store. Stella stepped swiftly aside, and Steve crashed straight into a model of Rudolph the Red-Nosed Reindeer, complete with flashing nose. It swayed, then fell, bringing the Christmas tree down, too. Decorations went flying, and waiting children ran away, shrieking, for safety.

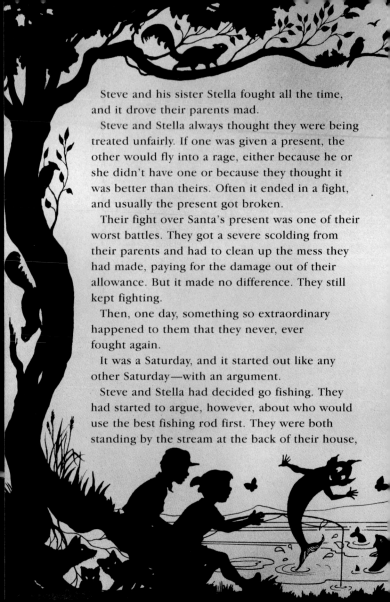

Steve and his sister Stella fought all the time,
and it drove their parents mad.

Steve and Stella always thought they were being
treated unfairly. If one was given a present, the
other would fly into a rage, either because he or
she didn't have one or because they thought it
was better than theirs. Often it ended in a fight,
and usually the present got broken.

Their fight over Santa's present was one of their
worst battles. They got a severe scolding from
their parents and had to clean up the mess they
had made, paying for the damage out of their
allowance. But it made no difference. They still
kept fighting.

Then, one day, something so extraordinary
happened to them that they never, ever
fought again.

It was a Saturday, and it started out like any
other Saturday—with an argument.

Steve and Stella had decided go fishing. They
had started to argue, however, about who would
use the best fishing rod first. They were both
standing by the stream at the back of their house,

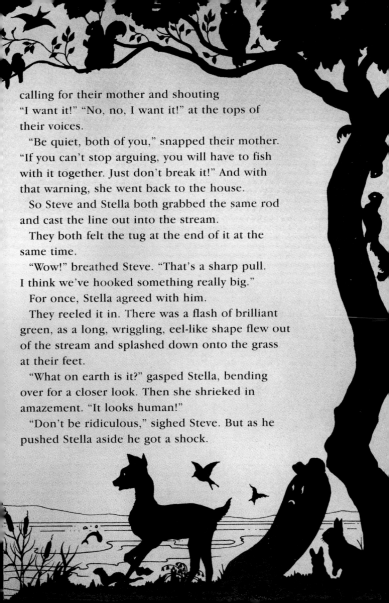

calling for their mother and shouting
"I want it!" "No, no, I want it!" at the tops of
their voices.

"Be quiet, both of you," snapped their mother.
"If you can't stop arguing, you will have to fish
with it together. Just don't break it!" And with
that warning, she went back to the house.

So Steve and Stella both grabbed the same rod
and cast the line out into the stream.

They both felt the tug at the end of it at the
same time.

"Wow!" breathed Steve. "That's a sharp pull.
I think we've hooked something really big."

For once, Stella agreed with him.

They reeled it in. There was a flash of brilliant
green, as a long, wriggling, eel-like shape flew out
of the stream and splashed down onto the grass
at their feet.

"What on earth is it?" gasped Stella, bending
over for a closer look. Then she shrieked in
amazement. "It looks human!"

"Don't be ridiculous," sighed Steve. But as he
pushed Stella aside he got a shock.

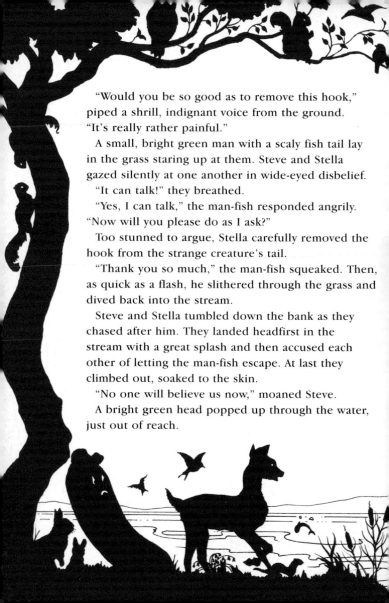

"Would you be so good as to remove this hook," piped a shrill, indignant voice from the ground. "It's really rather painful."

A small, bright green man with a scaly fish tail lay in the grass staring up at them. Steve and Stella gazed silently at one another in wide-eyed disbelief.

"It can talk!" they breathed.

"Yes, I can talk," the man-fish responded angrily. "Now will you please do as I ask?"

Too stunned to argue, Stella carefully removed the hook from the strange creature's tail.

"Thank you so much," the man-fish squeaked. Then, as quick as a flash, he slithered through the grass and dived back into the stream.

Steve and Stella tumbled down the bank as they chased after him. They landed headfirst in the stream with a great splash and then accused each other of letting the man-fish escape. At last they climbed out, soaked to the skin.

"No one will believe us now," moaned Steve.

A bright green head popped up through the water, just out of reach.

"I almost forgot," the man-fish called to them. "I grant you three wishes for catching me and then letting me go."

He disappeared beneath the water and was never seen again.

Steve and Stella looked at one another. Were they dreaming? Had they really been granted three wishes?

"I've read about this kind of thing in fairy stories," said Steve doubtfully. "But everyone knows that's all make-believe."

"Well, it can't be make-believe, can it?" Stella retorted. "What about the little green man? He was a fairy tale creature all right."

Steve agreed that they had actually hooked a creature that could talk and was half man and half fish. "But I bet you're wrong about the wishes," he scoffed.

"That's fine with me, Mr. Know-It-All," sneered Stella. "I'll take all three wishes. Now, what should I wish for first?"

"Oh no, you don't," said Steve, hurriedly putting a hand over her mouth to stop her.

Furious, Stella struggled away and tried to stop Steve from speaking. He pushed her away roughly, making her even more angry. Before they knew it, they had started fighting and the wishes went straight out of their heads.

Eventually, exhausted and feeling cold and hungry, Steve and Stella stopped fighting and flung themselves down on the grass.

"I'm starving!" complained Steve. "I wish I had a giant sausage to eat!"

There was a flash of bright green light, and an enormous, delicious-smelling fried sausage appeared, right beside him.

Steve and Stella stared at it, unable to believe their eyes and too amazed to speak.

Stella was the first to recover.

"You silly idiot! You've wasted a precious wish!" she screamed at her brother, beside herself with rage. "I wish you were that stupid sausage! That would teach you a lesson!"

Stella froze in horror, realizing—too late—what she had just done. With a bright green flash, her brother turned into a giant sausage.

It was an astonishing sight—a sausage the size of a tree trunk lying on the grass beside her. The sausage was dressed in the tatters of Steve's clothes. His baseball cap was now perched on one end of the sausage, which made it look even more ridiculous.

Then it started moaning.

"Help me! I don't want to be a sausage!" came the faint sound of Steve's voice from deep down inside the sausage.

For the first time in her life, Stella felt sorry for her brother.

"I don't want you to be a sausage, either," she said. "I wish you were Steve again."

There was a bright green flash. The sausage vanished, and Steve was lying on the grass next to her again.

"Oooh, that was really scary," he said. "Thanks for wishing me back."

"I missed you," Stella smiled.

"I missed you, too," grinned Steve.

And they really meant it. They started to enjoy each other's company and found that it was actually more fun *not* to fight. Their parents were so pleased that Steve and Stella had stopped arguing that they weren't angry about the state they were in when they came back from their fishing expedition—nor about the silly story they told about a little green man-fish and three wishes.

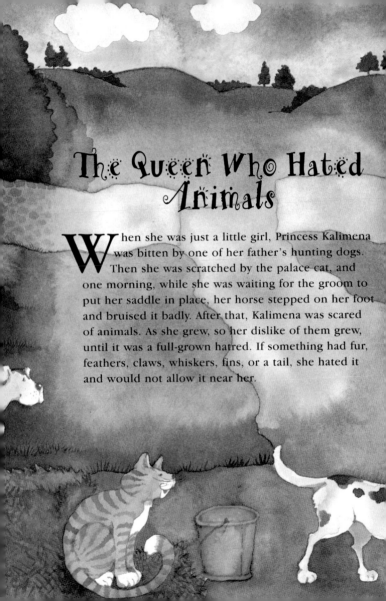

The Queen Who Hated Animals

When she was just a little girl, Princess Kalimena was bitten by one of her father's hunting dogs. Then she was scratched by the palace cat, and one morning, while she was waiting for the groom to put her saddle in place, her horse stepped on her foot and bruised it badly. After that, Kalimena was scared of animals. As she grew, so her dislike of them grew, until it was a full-grown hatred. If something had fur, feathers, claws, whiskers, fins, or a tail, she hated it and would not allow it near her.

So when Princess Kalimena became Queen Kalimena, the first thing she did was pass a very unpopular new law.

"From this day forth, all animals are banned from the land," she declared.

Now, this was not too difficult to do in the palace grounds. The horses were removed from their stables, the dogs were taken out of their cozy kennels, and the peacocks were banished from the gardens. But the servants in the palace had a terrible time. Spiders were brushed from the corners, shutters were closed against stray bees, but no matter what they did, pill bugs always found a way in.

Out in the kingdom, it was even harder to banish the animals. The people needed their sheep and pigs, and their cows and chickens, and they loved their pets. And how could they possibly banish the birds and snakes, butterflies and rabbits? It was a silly law made by a silly queen, they thought.

However, silly as she was, the queen was very powerful and had to be obeyed. So the people found

a way around the problem. They kept the animals, but disguised them as other things so that the queen and her officials would never know that they were still there.

One day, Queen Kalimena decided to take a tour of her land. She rumbled along the country lanes in her carriage, pulled very slowly by four very hot and tired guards.

"Can't you go any faster?" she yelled.

The queen waved to her subjects as they worked in the fields and she was pleased to see that there were no animals. However, some of the people did look very strange. Their clothes didn't fit them well at all, and they didn't seem to be doing very much work. And once, when she was passing a hairy-looking scarecrow, she was convinced she heard it bleat like a goat.

When she got hungry, the queen stopped at the nearest house to have lunch. On this particular day, it was the house that belonged to Tasha and her family.

"The queen is coming," warned her father as he rushed into the house. "Are the animals hidden?"

"Yes," replied Tasha. "Just throw the tablecloth over the pig and we'll be ready."

"Now, stand very still," she said to the rabbits on the shelves who were pretending to be bookends. "And you two," she said to the cranes in the corner, "you're supposed to be lamps, remember, so no squawking."

The queen strode in haughtily.

"Your Majesty," said Tasha's mother, curtsying. "How lovely to see you."

"Oh, what a gorgeous shawl," said the queen, looking at two white swans that Tasha's father had hung on a hook with strict instructions not to flap their wings. The queen picked up the swans and draped them over her shoulders. "Oh, it fits me beautifully," she said. "So warm, and surprisingly heavy."

She sat down.

Now, the chair that the queen sat in was really a kangaroo with a cloth thrown over him, and when she sat down he did his best not to gasp or fidget. Tasha's mother put a wonderful spread of food on the table, which was actually the pig, and the queen started to eat and drink.

Tasha and her mother and father watched nervously. Suddenly there was a bleating cry from outside, and a thump. One of the sheep, which the farmers had put into the trees to make them look like low-lying clouds, had fallen to the ground.

"What was that?" asked the queen, looking up from her meal.

"Oh, just the baby," said Tasha's mother. "He must have fallen out of his crib again. I'll go and put him back."

Just then, a hedgehog wandered out from under a chair and stopped in the middle of the floor.

"What is that?" asked the queen. "It looks like a hedge..."

"Oh, my brush," said Tasha. "I wondered where that had gone." And she picked up the hedgehog, turned it upside down and started brushing her hair with it. "I hate to have tangled hair, don't you, Your Majesty?"

"Indeed," said the queen, eyeing Tasha suspiciously. "Is there any pepper?" she asked.

"Here, Your Majesty," said Tasha, placing her pet hamster in front of the queen. Hammie was wearing a little hat full of pepper with holes in the top, and he was standing as still and upright as he could, with his eyes closed.

"What a strange-looking pepper shaker," said the queen, picking up Hammie and shaking him vigorously. A cloud of pepper filled the room and Hammie sneezed.

"It sneezed!" cried the queen in alarm. "I am sure the pepper shaker sneezed!"

Then one of the rabbits moved. It wasn't his fault; the heavy books were leaning against him. As books tumbled off the shelf the rabbit leaped out of the way to avoid being squashed.

The queen screamed and turned to Tasha, her face red with rage.

"You know I have banned animals!" she yelled, and stamped her foot hard, right on the kangaroo's foot. That was enough for the poor kangaroo. He started bounding around the room, with the queen holding on for dear life. Squealing loudly, the pig ran off and the plates fell crashing to the floor. The cranes squawked and took off out the window, the lampshades still on their heads. The cat cushions leaped from the chairs, the snake draft stoppers slithered out the door, and the kangaroo bounded out of the house and made for the open country, with Queen Kalimena still clinging to him.

"Put me down!" screamed the queen, and finally the kangaroo did—but just then the swans decided it was time to get away.

They flapped their wings and took to the

air, taking the queen with them as they flew.
Higher and higher they soared.

"OHHH!" screamed the queen. Then "Oohh,"
in a slightly different voice. She was flying, which
was something she'd always wanted to do. The
swans took her high over her kingdom, beating
their great white wings, and the queen laughed
as she swooped low over the palace and the town.
When the swans finally brought the queen gently
down beside the lake, she was ecstatic.

Her court officials ran outside.

"Shoot the swans," one of them shouted.

"No," cried the queen. "Let them live. Let all
the animals live. They are wonderful."

So the swans returned to the lake, the rabbits
went back to their burrows, the sheep climbed
gratefully down from the trees, and they all
lived properly ever after.

Ice Cool Duel

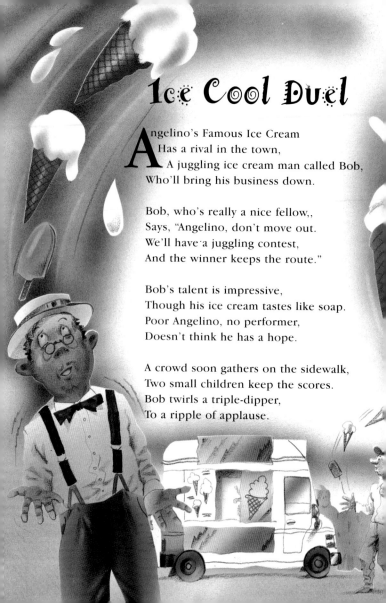

Angelino's Famous Ice Cream
Has a rival in the town,
A juggling ice cream man called Bob,
Who'll bring his business down.

Bob, who's really a nice fellow,,
Says, "Angelino, don't move out.
We'll have a juggling contest,
And the winner keeps the route."

Bob's talent is impressive,
Though his ice cream tastes like soap.
Poor Angelino, no performer,
Doesn't think he has a hope.

A crowd soon gathers on the sidewalk,
Two small children keep the scores.
Bob twirls a triple-dipper,
To a ripple of applause.

Angelino keeps his cool, though,
Knows that he will be just fine.
What goes up a plain old cone,
Comes down a lemon'n' lime.

Bob hates the thought of losing,
Reaches down toward his knees,
Pulls out a cherry-flavored ice pop,
Tells Angelino, "Time to *freeze*!"

But Angelino's wise to Bob,
So he plays his final trick.
Bob falls, knocked out cold,
By a large vanilla brick!

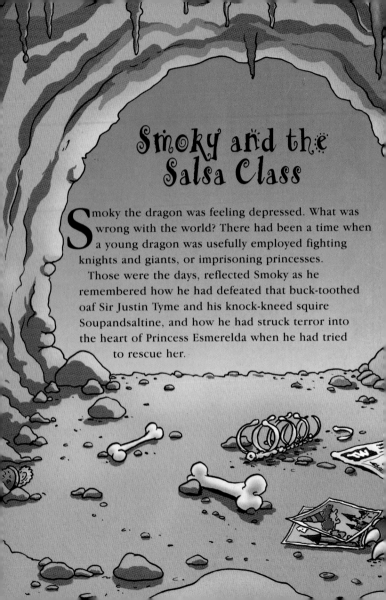

Smoky and the Salsa Class

Smoky the dragon was feeling depressed. What was wrong with the world? There had been a time when a young dragon was usefully employed fighting knights and giants, or imprisoning princesses.

Those were the days, reflected Smoky as he remembered how he had defeated that buck-toothed oaf Sir Justin Tyme and his knock-kneed squire Soupandsaltine, and how he had struck terror into the heart of Princess Esmerelda when he had tried to rescue her.

A tear rolled down Smoky's fat cheek as he lay on his back staring at the stalactites on the ceiling of his damp cave. His friends had stopped visiting now that he had no adventures to relate. Something stirred in the corner of the cave. It was Bernard, a mouse-eared bat who had moved into Smoky's cave without asking. He was inclined to give his opinion on anything and everything without being asked either.

Smoky sighed bitterly. "What you need is an accomplishment," Bernard pitched in from his corner. "You lie there all day dreaming about the past. No wonder people think you're boring! Why don't you take an evening class?" Smoky could see Bernard's tiny eyes glittering in the darkness, but it was disconcerting talking to Bernard when Bernard's eyes were where his mouth should be.

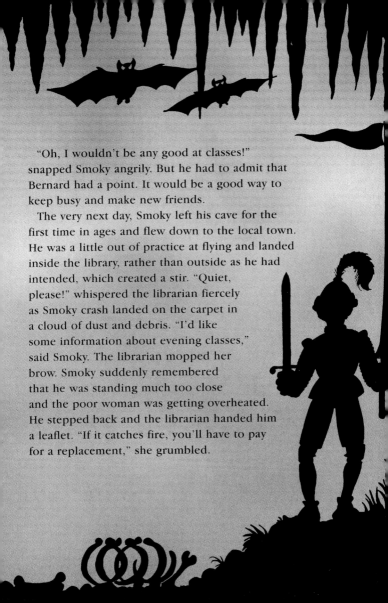

"Oh, I wouldn't be any good at classes!"
snapped Smoky angrily. But he had to admit that
Bernard had a point. It would be a good way to
keep busy and make new friends.

The very next day, Smoky left his cave for the
first time in ages and flew down to the local town.
He was a little out of practice at flying and landed
inside the library, rather than outside as he had
intended, which created a stir. "Quiet,
please!" whispered the librarian fiercely
as Smoky crash landed on the carpet in
a cloud of dust and debris. "I'd like
some information about evening classes,"
said Smoky. The librarian mopped her
brow. Smoky suddenly remembered
that he was standing much too close
and the poor woman was getting overheated.
He stepped back and the librarian handed him
a leaflet. "If it catches fire, you'll have to pay
for a replacement," she grumbled.

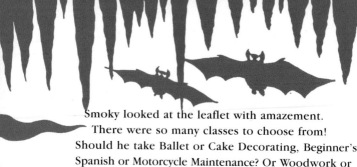

Smoky looked at the leaflet with amazement.
There were so many classes to choose from!
Should he take Ballet or Cake Decorating, Beginner's
Spanish or Motorcycle Maintenance? Or Woodwork or
Computer Studies? His head started to spin. Then he
remembered what Bernard had said. He needed an
accomplishment. Something to make him feel at ease
and confident at parties—should he be invited to any,
he thought wistfully.

Bernard was polishing off a fly sandwich
when Smoky got back to the cave that evening.
"I'm signing up for evening class," he announced.
"Really?" said Bernard between mouthfuls.
"Which one?"

"Salsa dancing!" cried Smoky, giving a little
twirl. "Salsa dancing?" squeaked Bernard.
"Salsa dancing?" And he laughed so much a
bit of sandwich went down (or maybe up) the
wrong way and he nearly fell off the cave wall.
When he'd stopped coughing and spluttering, and
had rearranged his wings, Bernard said in a
somewhat serious tone, "Don't forget to buy some
dancing shoes," and promptly fell asleep. Smoky
looked down at his large scaly feet and long sharp
claws, and wondered where he would find shoes
to fit.

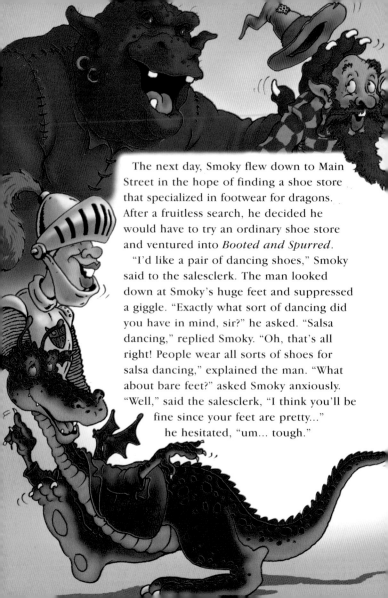

The next day, Smoky flew down to Main Street in the hope of finding a shoe store that specialized in footwear for dragons. After a fruitless search, he decided he would have to try an ordinary shoe store and ventured into *Booted and Spurred*.

"I'd like a pair of dancing shoes," Smoky said to the salesclerk. The man looked down at Smoky's huge feet and suppressed a giggle. "Exactly what sort of dancing did you have in mind, sir?" he asked. "Salsa dancing," replied Smoky. "Oh, that's all right! People wear all sorts of shoes for salsa dancing," explained the man. "What about bare feet?" asked Smoky anxiously. "Well," said the salesclerk, "I think you'll be fine since your feet are pretty..." he hesitated, "um... tough."

Before he knew it, it was time for Smoky to make his way to the community center for his first class. He felt nervous as he approached the room. What would people think of him? Would they mind dancing with a barefoot dragon? Maybe they'd all be scared and run away. He stepped into the room and looked around. Then his jaw dropped in amazement. The room was full of extraordinary folk all chattering away. There was a witch in conversation with a king, an ogre roaring with laughter and slapping an elf on the back, and a knight in full armor flirting with a princess.

"Welcome, welcome!" said a voice. "You're new, aren't you?" Smoky turned around to see the teacher approaching him with an outstretched hand.

He knew it must be the teacher because he was the only ordinary human in the room. He was dressed in tight black pants, a white shirt, and the shiniest black shoes that Smoky had ever seen. "I'm Mr. di Magico. What's your name?" asked the teacher. "Smoky," said Smoky.

"Well, Smoky," said Mr. di Magico, "We'll be starting in a minute, but please mingle first." And he went off to greet a timid-looking prince at the door.

Smoky heard a clattering noise as the knight struggled toward him. "Smoky, old pal!" boomed a pompous voice from under the visor. "Long time, no see!" Smoky was puzzled. He didn't recognize the voice. Then he caught sight of a set of buck teeth. It was Sir Justin Tyme! Smoky felt a little uneasy, remembering how savagely they

had once fought, and hung his head.
"Don't worry, old fellow!" chuckled Sir
Justin. "That was long ago. Now we're
all friends!" He clasped Smoky in a noisy
embrace. Smoky could feel bits of metal
sticking into him, but he didn't complain.
He was just glad to have a friend.

"Find a partner, everyone!" Mr. di Magico
called out, and clapped his hands. Smoky
hoped that he one of the pretty princesses
might be his partner but he was swept
onto the dance floor by a wild witch. He
didn't find the dancing easy, mainly because
he kept stepping on the witch's black boots
and leaving scratch marks with his claws.
At first he was worried that she might cast a
spell on him, but he soon realized that the
witch was enjoying herself, spinning
around so that her tattered black skirt flew.

"And change!" called Mr. di Magico. Suddenly, there was confusion as everyone changed partners. There was plenty of "Sorry, old fellow!" "May I...?" and "No, after you!" before Smoky found that he was now indeed dancing with one of the princesses. Not once did she look at Smoky. She kept her eyes fixed firmly on the floor and counted out the rhythm under her breath. Smoky decided that the witch was actually much more fun to dance with.

All too soon the class was over and Smoky flew back to his cave exhausted but happy. From the dark corner, Bernard opened one eye "How did it go?" he asked. "It was wonderful!" exclaimed Smoky. "I danced with three princesses, a queen, and a witch.

I think I'm in love with the witch," he added.

"Yes, yes," snapped Bernard impatiently. "But what about the salsa dancing?"

"Oh, the dancing," said Smoky sheepishly. "I wasn't very good at it. My big feet, you see. But they're having an end-of-term barbecue," he continued and started to grin. "And I'm certainly going to set that on fire!"

The Daffy Professor

"I've built my machine!" cried Professor Von Bean
"It's finished and ready to go!
The greatest invention I've had cause to mention!
It can trundle and suck, and it blows!

"The wheels are half green—the wildest you've seen!
The levers all stick out at the side!
It takes just one flick of the switch on this stick
And you'll hear all the gears go inside!

"It's got bright red stripes and lots of weird pipes
And things that light up on on the roof!
The coal goes in here and the smoke goes out there,
And instead of 'toot', it goes 'woof'!

"The door's made of glass, and the floor's made of gras
There are flowers and plants on the back!
There's a cupboard inside that's really quite wide,
So there's somewhere to store a snack!"

Von Bean was delighted and very excited
And happily burst into song.
But his assistant was flustered and suddenly blustered,
"I think that something is wrong!"

"I know I'm persistent!" cried Von Bean's young assistant
"And I love your machine through and through!
The lights flash on top when it spins and can't stop!
But what on earth does it DO?"

With a terrible cry and a long, drawn-out sigh,
Von Bean said, "Oh what a fool!
I never once thought— I've really been caught—
This machine does *nothing useful at all*!"

The Flying Contest

It was a hot day on the African savannah when the animals saw that a sign had been tacked to the trunk of a tree. They gathered around to read it.

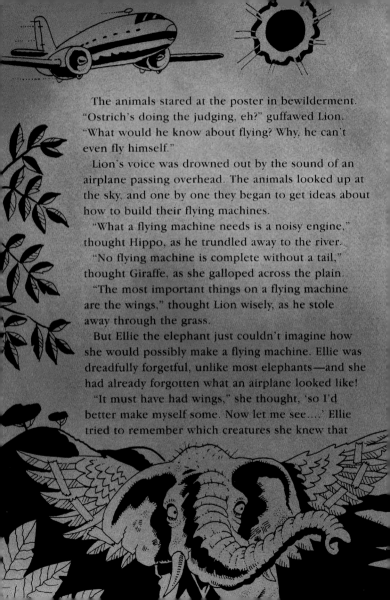

The animals stared at the poster in bewilderment. "Ostrich's doing the judging, eh?" guffawed Lion. "What would he know about flying? Why, he can't even fly himself."

Lion's voice was drowned out by the sound of an airplane passing overhead. The animals looked up at the sky, and one by one they began to get ideas about how to build their flying machines.

"What a flying machine needs is a noisy engine," thought Hippo, as he trundled away to the river.

"No flying machine is complete without a tail," thought Giraffe, as she galloped across the plain.

"The most important things on a flying machine are the wings," thought Lion wisely, as he stole away through the grass.

But Ellie the elephant just couldn't imagine how she would possibly make a flying machine. Ellie was dreadfully forgetful, unlike most elephants—and she had already forgotten what an airplane looked like!

"It must have had wings," she thought, 'so I'd better make myself some. Now let me see....' Ellie tried to remember which creatures she knew that

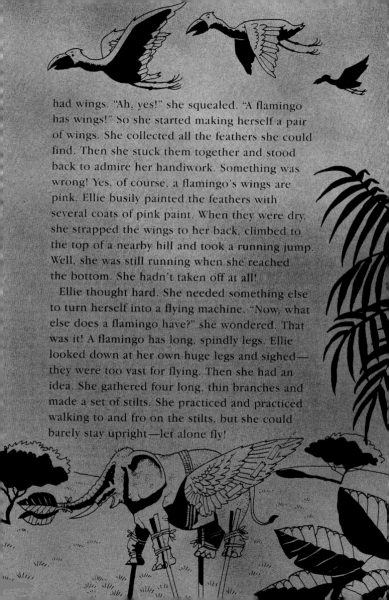

had wings. "Ah, yes!" she squealed. "A flamingo has wings!" So she started making herself a pair of wings. She collected all the feathers she could find. Then she stuck them together and stood back to admire her handiwork. Something was wrong! Yes, of course, a flamingo's wings are pink. Ellie busily painted the feathers with several coats of pink paint. When they were dry, she strapped the wings to her back, climbed to the top of a nearby hill and took a running jump. Well, she was still running when she reached the bottom. She hadn't taken off at all!

Ellie thought hard. She needed something else to turn herself into a flying machine. "Now, what else does a flamingo have?" she wondered. That was it! A flamingo has long, spindly legs. Ellie looked down at her own huge legs and sighed—they were too vast for flying. Then she had an idea. She gathered four long, thin branches and made a set of stilts. She practiced and practiced walking to and fro on the stilts, but she could barely stay upright—let alone fly!

Something was still wrong. Then Ellie remembered. A flamingo has a curved beak. She found two large leaves and bent them into a curved shape. Then she painted them pink and attached them to the end of her trunk, like a beak. But she still could not fly.

"It's obvious," thought Ellie unhappily, "that I'm too heavy to take off. I'll have to lose some weight before Saturday." So for the rest of the week, she gave up ice cream, cake and other fattening foods. "It'll be worth it," she thought, "if I lose enough weight to fly."

The day of the contest arrived, and the animals brought their machines out onto the savannah to show off their flying skills to Ostrich. There was a lot of tittering as Ellie emerged from behind a bush. She was an extraordinary sight as she teetered along on her stilts, with her pink wings and her flapping beak. She also looked a little ill.

"Are you feeling all right, Ellie?" asked her friend Wildebeest anxiously.

"Fine, thank you, dear," replied Ellie. "Just a little hungry."

"Let's begin!" snapped Ostrich. "Who's first?"

"I am!" cried Hippo, leaping into the seat of his machine. "What a flying machine needs is noise!" he shouted over the roar of the engine. It really was a magnificent machine. It looked a little like a lawn mower with huge, shiny pistons.

"Isn't there something missing?" mused Cheetah with a smile.

But Hippo wasn't listening. "Here we go!" he cried, letting out the throttle as the machine shot off across the savannah in a cloud of black smoke. Faster and faster went the machine, but it didn't take off, of course, because it had no wings.

"Ha, ha!" laughed the animals with glee, as it smashed into a tree and Hippo climbed out looking disgruntled.

"Who's next?" asked Ostrich.

"Oh, I am," said Giraffe. "What a flying machine really needs is a tail," she said, as she climbed into her machine. It was spectacular, with a gleaming metal tail standing proudly at the back. She cantered off across the savannah, four legs sticking out of the machine. Faster and faster she galloped, but she didn't take off, because it had no wings.

"Hee, hee!" giggled the animals, as Giraffe's legs got all tangled up and she collapsed in a dizzy heap.

"Who's next?" said Ostrich.

"Meee!" purred Lion smugly. "You foolish animals," he sneered. "What a flying machine needs is wings." And he leaped effortlessly into his machine. The animals gasped in awe. Lion's machine had a simply beautiful pair of silver wings stretching out on either side.

Faster and faster went Lion across the savannah, and it looked as if his machine really might take off. He gave a loud roar of triumph, and a fly flew into his gaping mouth. He coughed, lost control, and the machine careered off course and into a watering hole.

"Ha, ha, hee, hee!" bellowed the animals, as a very wet Lion crawled out of the water.

"Now, what about Ellie?" said Ostrich, wiping tears of mirth from his eyes. But Ellie was nowhere to be found. When she had seen the other animals' machines she had been so ashamed of her own efforts that she had crept away. Besides, she was feeling very hungry.

"I'll have a nice picnic by myself," she thought. She wrapped all her favorite foods in a tablecloth, tied it with string, and went off to find a quiet spot. She was munching a delicious jelly doughnut when suddenly there was a tremendous gust of wind. Before she

could escape, she felt herself being
lifted up in the tablecloth and carried high
above the trees. She struggled to free herself
and got all tangled up in the string.

Just then, the other animals felt the gust, too.
They looked up into the sky and stared in
amazement. They couldn't believe their eyes!
Ellie was floating down toward them with the
tablecloth and string acting as a parachute!

"Ellie, you're the winner!" announced Ostrich,
as she landed on the ground with a soft bump.
The other animals cheered and cheered. "It's
time to claim your prize—bring out the balloon
basket!" called Ostrich. Ellie tried to squeeze
her large frame into the basket, but it just
wouldn't fit.

"I'd miss you all anyway," she said. "Why don't
we have a picnic together instead? It just so
happens that I'm still hungry!" So that is exactly
what they all did.

The Singing Bank Robber

Bernie McTavish had had a bad day at the office. He hadn't really gotten anything done all day. Then his wife phoned to say that a pipe had burst under the hall floor. Everything was all right, but he would have to climb in through the window, because the furniture was in front of the door.

Bernie put the telephone down with a sigh and put on his black leather motorcycle gear. He couldn't see the bag he usually put his office clothes in, so he found an empty cash bag in the safe and stuffed them into that instead.

Then he set off for home on his motorcycle. It was a dark, damp night. He hadn't gone very far when the motorcycle coughed, juddered, and stopped. Bernie tried to start the engine again, but it was no use: it was broken. With another deep sigh, Bernie dismounted, tucked his helmet under his arm, and trudged home. It started to rain.

"Oh, nuts," said Bernie.

He was nearly home when he realized that he had a stone in his boot. It was hurting his foot and making him limp, but he couldn't be bothered to take it out, so he limped home, feeling very sorry for himself. When he got to the house, he eased open the living-room window, threw the cash bag inside, and then climbed stiffly in after it.

Now, what Bernie didn't realize is that, as he did this, he was being watched—by two policemen, in a car across the street.

"Suspicious behavior!" said one policeman.

"Yes," said the other. "And what's more, he looks just like that bank robber we're looking for."

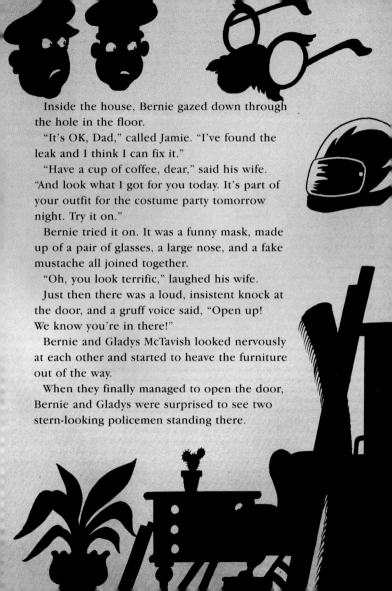

Inside the house, Bernie gazed down through the hole in the floor.

"It's OK, Dad," called Jamie. "I've found the leak and I think I can fix it."

"Have a cup of coffee, dear," said his wife. "And look what I got for you today. It's part of your outfit for the costume party tomorrow night. Try it on."

Bernie tried it on. It was a funny mask, made up of a pair of glasses, a large nose, and a fake mustache all joined together.

"Oh, you look terrific," laughed his wife.

Just then there was a loud, insistent knock at the door, and a gruff voice said, "Open up! We know you're in there!"

Bernie and Gladys McTavish looked nervously at each other and started to heave the furniture out of the way.

When they finally managed to open the door, Bernie and Gladys were surprised to see two stern-looking policemen standing there.

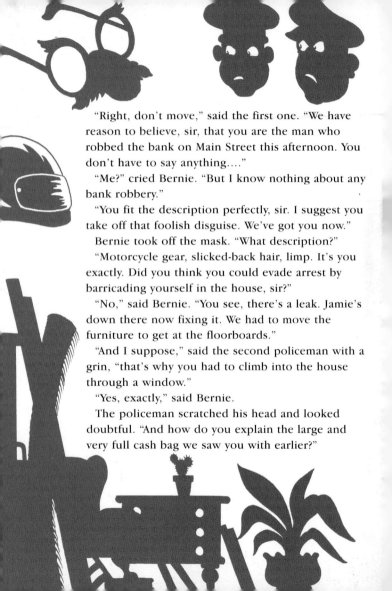

"Right, don't move," said the first one. "We have reason to believe, sir, that you are the man who robbed the bank on Main Street this afternoon. You don't have to say anything...."

"Me?" cried Bernie. "But I know nothing about any bank robbery."

"You fit the description perfectly, sir. I suggest you take off that foolish disguise. We've got you now."

Bernie took off the mask. "What description?"

"Motorcycle gear, slicked-back hair, limp. It's you exactly. Did you think you could evade arrest by barricading yourself in the house, sir?"

"No," said Bernie. "You see, there's a leak. Jamie's down there now fixing it. We had to move the furniture to get at the floorboards."

"And I suppose," said the second policeman with a grin, "that's why you had to climb into the house through a window."

"Yes, exactly," said Bernie.

The policeman scratched his head and looked doubtful. "And how do you explain the large and very full cash bag we saw you with earlier?"

"That was the suit that I wear in the office," said Bernie. "I always change before I come home. And my hair isn't slicked back, it's wet. I got caught in a heavy downpour."

"This all seems very unlikely, sir," said the first policeman. "How do you explain the bowling ball?"

"Bowling ball?"

"The robber threatened to knock over the bank staff with a bowling ball if they didn't hand over the cash. We clearly saw you with a bowling ball tucked under your arm, sir. You can't fool us."

For a moment Bernie didn't know what on earth they were talking about. Then his face brightened.

"Oh, no," he said. "That's not a bowling ball. That's my motorcycle helmet." He showed them the helmet.

"Ah-ha," said the policeman, as if he'd finally found the flaw in Bernie's argument. "But you arrived on foot."

"Yes, my bike broke down," said Bernie. "You see, there's an explanation for everything."

"And the limp?" asked the second policeman, looking more and more puzzled.

"A stone. In my boot," said Bernie. He took off his boot and held it upside down, and a tiny stone tinkled out onto the floor.

The first policeman whispered something to the second policeman. The second policeman looked doubtful for a moment and then said, "Could you sing for us, sir?"

"Sing?" said Bernie.

"Yes, sing a song for us."

"Anything in particular, Officer?" asked Bernie. He was beginning to think these two policemen were completely mad.

"Something from an opera, sir."

"But I don't know anything from an opera."

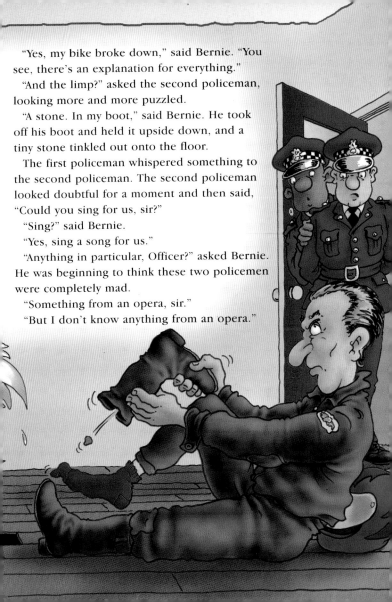

"Well, anything will do," said the second policeman.

Bernie took a deep breath and started to sing, "When the red, red, robin comes bob-bob-bobbing along...."

It sounded terrible. Bernie had never been much of a singer. He sounded like a cat stuck in a tree.

"Well, that's it," said the second policeman. "This is the wrong guy. He isn't the bank robber."

"It is?" said the first. "I mean, he isn't?"

"Yes, he isn't."

Everyone looked at the second policeman in complete bewilderment. "Why?" they asked.

"Well, while the staff was filling the cash bag, the robber was singing—something from an opera. And an eyewitness..."

"Or an earwitness," suggested Gladys.

"...an earwitness said he sounded good. Very good, in fact. So this man, who fits the description in every way, but sings like a parrot with a stomachache, can't possibly be him."

"My singing's not that bad," said Bernie.

"We're sorry to have troubled you, ma'am," said the first policeman, and as they turned to leave, he added, "I'd get this mess cleared up if I were you."

Bernie sat down heavily on an upside-down bucket and sighed. Could things possibly get worse? Just then Jamie appeared through the hole in the floor. He was dripping wet.

"I can't fix the leak, Dad," he said. "There's a lot of water coming in. Have you got a bucket?"

Bernie passed him his motorcycle helmet. "Use this," he sighed.

Did You Ever See?

Did you ever see a jester juggling with ice creams,
Or a pair of giant hamsters dueling with two chicken bones?
If you've never seen a crocodile eating Turkish taffy,
Then you, my friend, are totally and utterly quite daffy!

Did you ever see a puppy try to bake a lemon tart,
Or a pair of plump old ladies push a burglar in a cart?
If you've never seen an elephant sitting on a daisy,
Then you, my friend, are totally and utterly quite crazy!

Did you ever see a piglet all dressed up in polka dots,
Or a princess on her wedding day break out in bright green spots?
If you've never been out walking with a pink giraffe who's Sad,
Then you, my friend, are totally and utterly quite mad!

Did you ever see a colonel drinking coffee with a horse,
Or a three-legged mongoose? It's very rare, of course.
If you've never seen a witch's toad looking rather natty,
Then you, my friend, are totally and utterly quite batty!

Did you ever see a singing worm climbing up a wall,
Or a judge stand up in court and catch a purple tennis ball?
If you've never seen a kangaroo asleep in silk pajamas,
Then you, my friend, are totally and utterly quite bananas!

Did you ever see a king and queen drink watermelon tea,
Or a whale and several dolphins leaping out of your TV?
If you've never played the banjo with a very smelly cod,
Then you, my friend, are totally and utterly quite odd!

I know people think I'm mad, but here's my explanation—
I like to make up lots of stuff with my wild imagination!

The Dog Who Couldn't Bark

Ben gazed into a pair of large brown eyes, and the large brown eyes gazed back. It was a good face, friendly and intelligent, the sort of face that promised fun. Ben liked it immediately. Even though there were seven puppies to choose from, Ben knew that the little brown-and-white one with the funny ears and the curly tail was the one for him.

The puppy began to chase round and round in circles; then he rolled over a couple of times as Ben looked on in amusement and admiration.

"I think I like this one best," announced Ben as the puppy grabbed the sleeve of his jacket and began to tug at it playfully. Ben's dad frowned. Besides being the smallest in the litter by far, the puppy had a floppy ear that fell over his eye, while the other stuck straight up in the air. And his tail curled round and round, just like a pig's. "He's kind of small," Ben's dad pointed out, and the little puppy doubled his height by standing on his back legs and springing around the kitchen as if he were on a pogo stick.

"Please…" said Ben, as the puppy jumped up and tried to nibble his nose.

"Oh all right," agreed Ben's dad, seeing that the two were already inseparable. "But he has to be a watchdog not just a pet."

The puppy bared his teeth and made the most fearsome and ferocious face he could.

"Oh look," said Ben, giggling. "He's smiling."

"Has he got a good bark?" asked Ben's dad,

Beware of the Dog

making out a check and handing it over to Mrs. Walker, the woman selling the pups. She smiled broadly. "Well it's the strangest thing. He doesn't bark at all. I don't think he can."

Ben's dad was still shaking his head when the three of them got home.

"A six-inch-high watchdog, with a ridiculous tail, a floppy ear, and no bark," he complained to Ben's mom as she watched Ben and his new best friend race around the yard.

"Well, Ben certainly seems to like him," she remarked. And Ben certainly did.

It didn't take long for the new puppy to settle down. Ben gave him the name Jake, which sort of suited him. Jake was having the time of his life— a comfy new basket, an elegant tartan collar with his name on it, an enormous yard and a wonderful family. He tried very hard to please them all, especially Ben's dad. He handed him the hammer when he was putting the *Beware of the Dog* sign on the gate. He hadn't meant to drop it on his toe, of course, but it was kind of heavy for a small dog.

He also helped with the gardening, doing a lot of digging and rearranging the flower beds. After that Ben's dad had been so delighted that he had shut Jake in the back porch so he could have a nice long rest in his basket—digging was hard work, especially when you only had short legs.

And Jake really loved his basket. But, as the weeks rolled by and winter approached, it occurred to him that he might be warmer and even more comfortable if he took his beautiful gray blanket and put it on the living room sofa—after all, Ben's dad spent many a happy hour there.

It wasn't easy dragging the heavy blanket down the hall, but eventually he got there—just in time to see two men climbing in through the lounge window.

"Hey, they've got a dog," said the first man, whose name was Stan, as he shone a flashlight in Jake's bewildered face.

"That would explain the sign on the gate," replied the second man, whose name was Eric, as he tumbled headfirst through the window.

"What sign?" asked Stan, who could not read.

"The one that said *Beware of the Dog*," said Eric, putting his cap back on his head.

"Nice doggie, good doggie," began Stan. He approached Jake, who cocked his head to one side and wagged his tail.

"It's okay, he's friendly," said Stan. Eric tiptoed over, but didn't see Jake's blanket strewn across the middle of the floor and fell flat on his face. Jake licked his ear. "Get away," said Eric, trying not to laugh, even though he was fairly ticklish.

"Shhh," Stan said, and then pointed to a cabinet in the corner of the room. "The family silver," he added, rubbing his gloved hands together. Jake stared inquisitively at the two men. They looked a little strange in their striped sweaters and the peculiar masks that covered their eyes. He wanted to bark, but of course he couldn't, so he just watched as both men began to fill a large sack with Ben's dad's golf trophies. Jake instinctively knew that this wasn't right, strangers tiptoeing around in the middle of the night, helping themselves to whatever they liked. He ran toward Stan and grabbed the seat of his pants firmly in his teeth. "Get 'im off me," said Stan in a loud whisper, but Jake would not let go. Eric grabbed the dog by his back legs and pulled and pulled until there was a rrrrrrrrrip.

Stan's pants tore to reveal a pair of red-and-white polka-dot boxer shorts. Eric landed with a loud thud on the floor.

"Shhhhh…" said Stan, a little too loudly, but upstairs no one stirred.

Jake ran round and round in circles. He knew he had to make some noise, so he opened his mouth to bark, but all that came out was a weak little whimper. Then everything went black as Stan threw the blanket over him.

Jake wriggled and squirmed and squirmed and wriggled until he saw a scrap of light appear. Then he wriggled towards it until his nose peeped out.

"Up there," said Stan pointing to the top of the piano. Just as Eric grasped the magnificent silver candelabra, Jake leaped onto the piano stool and then onto the piano, trotting up and down the keys and creating the loudest and most terrible noise imaginable. Within seconds every light in the house seemed to be switched on and the sound of footsteps could be heard on the stairs.

"Run," shouted Eric, dropping the candelabra and the contents of the sack on the floor and

the two men fled through the open window.

When Ben's dad opened the living room door, he couldn't believe his eyes. The sack lay discarded on the floor with all his prized golf trophies spilling out of it, while little Jake ran up and down the piano keys wagging his curly tail frantically.

Ben and his mom came into the room. "What on earth happened in here?" asked Ben's mom, looking worried.

"It seems we had intruders," explained Ben's dad. He walked over to Jake and scratched him behind his ears. "But our watchdog here raised the alarm." Ben and his mom ran over to congratulate the clever, courageous little puppy, and Jake played an encore, dancing up and down the keys until everyone was laughing, holding on to their ears and begging him to stop.

"I think," began Ben's dad lifting Jake down, "I prefer Bach!"

I Wish...

I wish I was an elephant,
'Cause it would make me laugh.
To use my nose like a rubber hose
To rinse off in the bath.

I wish I was a chameleon,
Chameleons are best.
I'd change my color and life would be fuller,
For a change is as good as a rest.

I wish I was a hippo,
A hippo's life seems good.
They don't go to school, but keep nice and cool
Playing around in the mud.

I wish I was a dolphin,
A dolphin would be my wish.
Leaping and splashing, I'd be very dashing,
And swim along with the fish.

I wish I was an ostrich,
An ostrich would be grand.
But if I got scared, would I be prepared
To bury my head in the sand?

I wish I had more wishes,
But now my game is through,
I'm happy to be, quite simply me,
Enjoying a day at the zoo.

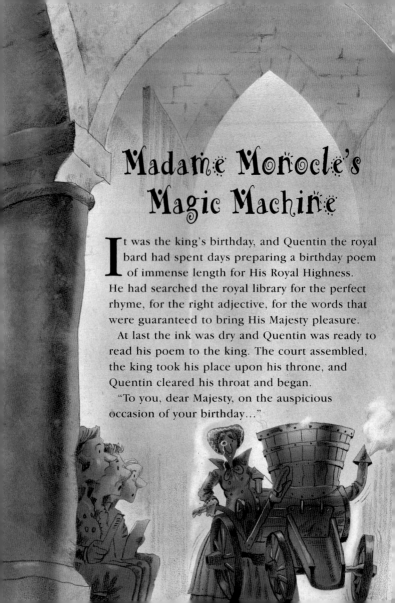

Madame Monocle's Magic Machine

I t was the king's birthday, and Quentin the royal bard had spent days preparing a birthday poem of immense length for His Royal Highness. He had searched the royal library for the perfect rhyme, for the right adjective, for the words that were guaranteed to bring His Majesty pleasure.

At last the ink was dry and Quentin was ready to read his poem to the king. The court assembled, the king took his place upon his throne, and Quentin cleared his throat and began.

"To you, dear Majesty, on the auspicious occasion of your birthday…"

He began to read his verse in a loud and pompous voice. At first the king looked attentive. Then he noticed that Quentin was holding a great many sheets of paper—and was still only on page one! "Oh dear," thought the king. "I wish I hadn't eaten so much. I'm feeling rather sleepy." His eyelids drooped.

"...my king so fair
   with lustrous hair...." Quentin was saying.

Soon the king was asleep and snoring gently. The queen was just wondering whether to wake her husband, when there was a commotion outside the throne room and in burst an old woman. She dragged a brightly painted, clattering machine behind her that made greasy black tire marks on the marble floor as she pushed her way through the throng toward the royal throne.

"Wake up, Reggie!" hissed the queen, poking the king in the ribs with a long, red fingernail. "You must do something!"

"Eh? What? I'll teach that two-headed Martian a lesson!" shouted the king, who was dreaming that he'd been abducted by aliens. He sat bolt upright and stared at the old woman.

"Who...?" he began.

"How dare...?" started Quentin. But the old lady interrupted them both.

"I am Madame Monocle," she announced, "and this is my Magic Recycling Machine. Feed it your unwanted bits and pieces, your odds and ends, and watch them become transformed into fabulous, new, and truly useful items before your very eyes!" She did a little pirouette before the king and ended with a curtsy.

The king was just about to have Madame Monocle and her filthy machine thrown out, when he remembered how much Quentin's poem had bored him. This might be much more interesting!

The king didn't believe Madame Monocle for a
minute, but he thought it would be amusing to see
what happened next.

"Very well," he said. "What can your machine do?"

"What do you say we begin with a royal sock?" said
Madame Monocle, reaching down to unbuckle the
king's shoe. The court froze. What would the king do?
Touching the royal foot was unthinkable! To everyone's
utter amazement, the king sat quite meekly while
Madame Monocle removed his sock, exposing five pink
toes for all the world to see.

The court gasped as the old woman reached up and
lifted a lid on top of the machine. In went the sock and
up went a plume of purple smoke before she slammed
the lid down again. Madame Monocle stood smiling
sweetly as the machine began to make the most
fearsome and embarrassing noises. It shook and
steamed and gurgled and belched, until finally out of a
chute at one side slid a beautiful woolen scarf!

The king looked astonished as Madame Monocle stepped forward and arranged the scarf around his neck. Then he smiled and said, "Who else has something to recycle?"

A courtier passed the old lady a newspaper. She stuffed it into the machine, and a few moments later out shot an elegant wooden candlestick. The court cheered. Everyone was fascinated by the extraordinary machine as more objects were fed into it. Everyone, that is, except for one person.

In all the excitement, nobody noticed the look of fury on Quentin's face. "My day has been ruined!" he thought angrily. "They didn't listen to the end of my wonderful poem! I'll make them regret it!" He slipped round the back of the machine and twiddled a few knobs. Nobody noticed. They were too busy watching to see what would come out next. Madame Monocle had just thrown a chicken bone into the machine.

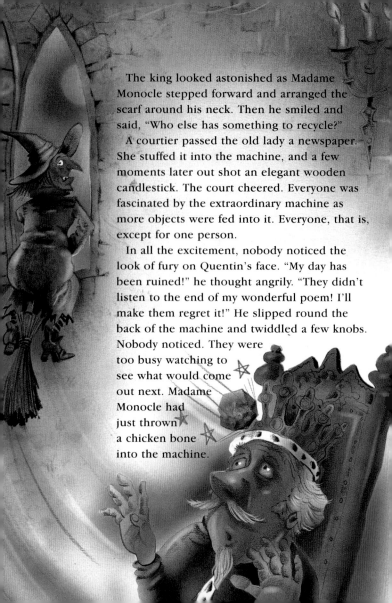

All eyes were on the chute.

Suddenly there was a dreadful cackling noise and out of the chute shot an old crone on a broomstick. She had a stone in her fist, which she hurled straight at the king. He ducked as the stone smashed into his crown. Before anyone could stop her, the crone and had escaped out the window.

"Stop the machine!" screamed the queen. But it was too late. Madame Monocle had already fed her gold ring into the machine. The contraption hissed and then began spitting out pieces of knotted old string.

There was a stunned silence. "I don't know what could have happened! It's very strange!" said Madame Monocle.

The king stood up, purple-faced with rage. "You've ruined my birthday!" he yelled. "Take her away, guards!"

"Wait!" shouted the queen. "I know your game," she continued, pointing her finger at Quentin, who was smirking in the corner. "Bone, crone, stone! Ring, string! Obviously our precious court poet has turned the machine into a ridiculous rhymer!"

"Bring him here!" commanded the king. The guards, who had Madame Monocle in a tight grip, dropped their hold. They surrounded Quentin and dragged him in front of the king.

"Well?" demanded the king.

At first Quentin denied everything. But at last he had to admit that he had tampered with the machine. He told the king how hurt he was that no one had wanted to listen to his poem.

The king looked thoughtful. He whispered something to the queen, who thought for a moment and then nodded. Finally, he said to Quentin, "Although you have greatly displeased us, nevertheless the queen and I are forced to admire your skill at producing rhymes out of this machine. As punishment, you will feed it your own work, and we'll see what comes out!"

Reluctantly, Quentin fed sheet after sheet of his poem into the machine. After much whirring, down the chute came a scrap of paper with a few lines of writing on it. Quentin picked it up.

"Well?" said the king.

"It's not quite what I would have liked...." said Quentin hesitantly.

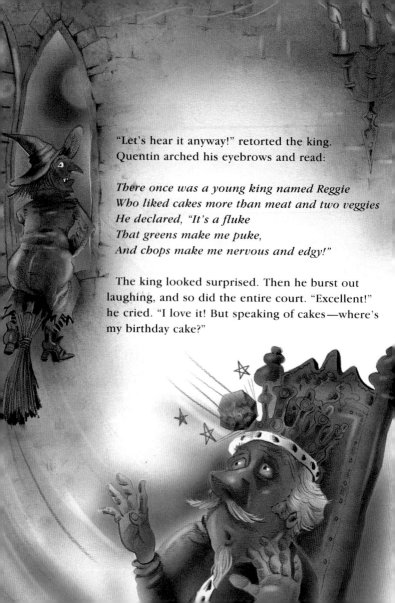

"Let's hear it anyway!" retorted the king. Quentin arched his eyebrows and read:

There once was a young king named Reggie
Who liked cakes more than meat and two veggies
He declared, "It's a fluke
That greens make me puke,
And chops make me nervous and edgy!"

The king looked surprised. Then he burst out laughing, and so did the entire court. "Excellent!" he cried. "I love it! But speaking of cakes—where's my birthday cake?"

There was an awkward silence in court.
Then Madame Monocle stepped forward.

"Perhaps I can help," she said, as she
fed a box of matches into the machine.
Presto—out came a chocolate cake with
candles blazing on it!

"My best birthday ever!" beamed the
king, as he blew out his candles.

There Was an Old Woman

There was an old woman
Who lived on our street.
You wouldn't believe all
The things she could eat.

For breakfast each morning,
A full three-course meal
Of nuts and bolts served in
A bicycle wheel!

She always was careful
Not to miss lunch.
On brooms, mops, and buckets
She'd nibble and crunch.

Trumpets and trombones were
Her favorite dinner,
But though always eating,
She kept getting thinner.

At midnight she'd snack on
Some bees in their hives,
All swiftly washed down with
The forks, spoons, and knives!

What would finish her off
No one could have known—
For that nutty, old woman
Choked on a fish bone!